TATTOO

The Mark of the Feathered Serpent

JUAN BÚTTO

DEDICATION

This book is dedicated to my wife Becky, the co-creator of this story and the author of our love story for over forty years.

The Mark of the Feathered Serpent

ACKNOWLEDGMENTS

Kate Farmer
Artwork and Illustrations

Gena Marlin
Creative Director

Special thanks go out to my Beta Readers:

Madison Cruz
Camille Gros
Marie Oliver
Angel Rodriguez
Joshua Villemaire

Their input was valuable and appreciated.

I would also like to especially thank **Stephen Arseneault**, author of the Science Fiction Novels: Sodium Series, AMP Series, Omega Series, Hadron Series, Arms Series and Freedom Series for technical consulting and creative input.

Finally, thanks to the many people who have encouraged and supported me along the way.

Prologue

As the morning sun struggled to shine through the thick jungle foliage, the War Lord Yax Mo is leading twenty battle-hardened Mayan warriors through the morning mist to Copan. It has taken the Mayans two and a half days through the jungle to reach Copan from Tikal. Yax Mo is sponsored by the King of Tikal, and his orders are to take Copan by military force and subjugate the residents.

From a hill overlooking the city, Yax Mo could see a flurry of activity. The people of Copan had gotten word of the approaching army, and were desperately preparing to defend the city. Copan warriors and hunters gathered their weapons together and encircled the village, waiting for the onslaught they knew was coming.

The Copan militia had sixty-men to defend the village against twenty Mayan warriors, but the Mayans wore *The Mark of the Feathered Serpent*, tattooed on the inside of each man's forearm. It connected the warrior's spirit with the spirit of Kukulkan, the Mayan god of war; and endowed the wearer with the strength and speed of the jungle cats. They were virtually unbeatable in battle.

As Yax Mo and his warriors attacked, they terrified the Copan militia with a battle cry that shook the soul of even the bravest warrior, and many of the Copan militia abandoned their posts and ran.

The village was in complete pandemonium. Mayan warriors poured in, killing the Copan militia and anyone else who resisted. The Mayans were armed with spiked clubs for breaking bones and smashing skulls. They also had short-blade swords for stabbing at close range. Some of Yax Mo's warriors carried spears and shields, and all of his men had some form of poison darts.

The air was filled with the sounds of mothers screaming, babies crying, and the smell of death as the Mayans brutalized the Copan militia. Men moaned and screamed out in pain as they lay on the ground dying. The fighting was hand-to-hand, and the Mayan warriors preformed acts of great bravery in the hope of being recognized for their courage and skill in battle.

The attack lasted less than thirty-minutes; and when it was over, the survivors were rounded up and driven to the center of the village. There they were separated into three groups. The remaining Militia and any other resisters were grouped together and led away to be sacrificed to Kukulkan, the god of war. The second group was made up of those who would be enslaved. And the third group was made up of those who were submissive and presented no threat to the Mayans. These residents would be allowed to stay because Yax Mo knew his new city would need residents to help build the temples and other structures.

He legitimized his claim to the throne by marrying into the old Copán royal family, and was elevated to kingship by his sponsors in Tikal. He founded a dynasty that lasted for over four hundred years and produced sixteen kings.

Copan became the art and religious center of the Mayan universe. Sacred plants and flowers grew for miles in every direction. But the worst drought in a thousand years, combined with perpetual warfare among the Mayan city states caused the collapse of the Mayan civilization.

Faced with starvation, most of the Mayans left in search of food. However, some stayed and melted into the jungle where they continue to practice the old ways in secret.

There are events in everyone's life that shape their future.
The key is to recognize them and to embrace the change.
-Juan Bútto

    Luke heard a knock at the door. By the time he got there the UPS man was just pulling away, but he had left a package at the doorstep. When he reached down to pick it up, Luke noticed that it was addressed to his wife Stacy; so he carried it into the house, laid it on the kitchen table, and went back to doing the dishes.

    When he set the package on the table, he noticed it was from Stacy's Uncle Robert, a professor of Archeology at the University of Miami, and part of an international team working on the excavation of the ancient Mayan ruins at Copan. He had been living deep in the mountain jungles of western Honduras for the past five months and was preparing to return home when the rainy season started in November.

Luke had just finished filling the dishwasher when the phone rang. It was Stacy. She was leaving the doctor's office, and was calling from the car. She was seven-months pregnant with twins, and had the pregnant glow he had heard about his whole life.

"Hey baby."

"Hi Stacy, how'd it go?"

"It couldn't be better. The babies are doing fine and I'm feeling great. What are you doing?"

"I just finished the dishes, and was thinking maybe we'll go out for dinner when you get back."

"That would be great," she said. "I should be home in about twenty-minutes."

"Ok, and by the way, you got a package from your Uncle Robert."

"Really, that's great. What's in the package?"

"I don't know. It's addressed to you, so I didn't open it."

"Well, we'll check it out as soon as I get home," she said.

"Ok, but you better hurry, the suspense is killing me," Luke replied. Then he shook the package near the phone where Stacy could hear it, and they both laughed.

Even though they had been married for over four

years, Luke was just as crazy about her now as he was when they first met at a Tattoo convention.

The Miami Tattoo Convention took place in mid-November that year, and Luke had rented an artist's booth for several years in a row. His work was in demand and he stayed very busy. It was also a chance for him to visit with tattoo artists from all over the country.

On the last day of the convention, Stacy Noland walked into his life.

Stacy was in her early twenties, with soft red hair and captivating brown eyes. She wore a sage green tee-shirt that was open in the back to reveal a large geometric tattoo. She also wore a pair of cutoff shorts that were hard to ignore, and revealed a floral tattoo on each leg that started at the top of her hips and ran down her legs, stopping just short of her ankle.

Luke caught a glimpse of her out of the corner of his eye. He stopped what he was doing to turn around and check her out, and when they made eye contact, they connected immediately.

"Hi, I'm Stacy." she said.

"Hi." he replied as he stood up to greet her. "I'm Luke."

Just then he noticed Marti, who he knew from his Tattoo Shop, and realized the two girls were together.

"Hi," she said as she reached over to hug him.

"This must be the cousin from Atlanta you've been telling me about." Luke said, and then turned his attention back to Stacy. "How are you two related?"

"Marti's father is my Dad's brother, and since my father passed away a couple of years ago, my Uncle Robert has been there for me. He's like a second father to me."

"Yeah, I understand from Marti he's a great guy, very intellectual. And as far as I can see he only has one flaw, he's not a tattoo lover. He gives Marti a hard time about her tattoos. But hey, nobody's perfect" Luke joked, and they all laughed.

"Actually, I did both of Marti's tattoos," he added.

"Well, they're both beautiful," Stacy replied.

"Thanks. Hey, have you had a chance to check out the Miami night life yet?"

"Not yet. Marti's only nineteen. She can't get into any of the clubs, so I'm still hoping to find someone who can show me around."

"Well, your search is over." Luke said. "Why don't you let me take you to dinner and we can check out some clubs afterwards if you'd like?"

Well, Stacy couldn't say yes fast enough, and from then on, they were inseparable. She spent every day with him for the rest of the time she was in Miami. Call it chemistry, call it lust; whatever you call it, they had it bad.

It wasn't long before Stacy relocated to Miami. She moved in with her cousin Marti and her Uncle Robert, and went to work with Luke in his shop. They fell deeply in love and were married. They had a romantic ceremony on the beach, and a dream Honeymoon to Jamaica as a gift from Stacy's Uncle.

Luke continued reminiscing and piddling around the kitchen, keeping one eye on the mysterious package, and the other eye on the clock, anxiously waiting for Stacy to get home. Suddenly, his train of thought was interrupted when he heard Stacy's car pull up into the driveway, and he met her at the door.

"I'm glad you're home. I've been dying to know what's in that package."

"Me too," she said, as she walked into the kitchen and found the package on the table.

Stacy got a knife and cut the box open. Inside she found a leather binder that contained a letter from her Uncle, as well as some pictures of temple carvings and native tattoos. But before she had a chance to read the letter, they both got a look at the photographs and gasped.

They looked at each other in bewilderment, not totally understanding what they were looking at. The tattoos were breathtaking. The colors seemed alive. They were glowing, and literally jumped off the page. They were the most beautiful tattoos either one of them had ever seen. Stacy and Luke were both speechless until she picked up the letter and read it out loud.

Dear Stacy,

The last four months have been amazing. Now that we've broken the Mayan code, we're able to translate writings left behind that were previously a mystery.

One of the things we found at the Temple of Kukulkan is an inscription about a warrior cult and a magic tattoo. It connected the warrior's spirit with Kukulkan, the Mayan god of war, and endowed the warrior with super human abilities.

I've enclosed photographs of several men from remote mountain villages I've encountered. Their tattoos are quite extraordinary. It may have something to do with the formula for tattoo ink we found on the temple wall. It looks like part of the formula is missing, but I sent you what we have so far because I know your professional curiosity will be aroused.

I'm hoping to finish the translation before I leave, and will let you know if I find anything else.

Love,

Uncle Robert

Later that evening, all they talked about at dinner was the tattoo ink.

"I'd love to talk to your Uncle Robert. When did he say he was coming home?"

"Not until sometime in November, about five or six weeks from now. Hopefully he'll be home in time for his birthday. Marti said that they can only stay in the jungle for about six months at a time, until the rainy season starts." Stacy continued.

"Where do they stay when they're down there?" Luke questioned.

"They have trailers located in a base camp. They travel to the site of the dig every day in trucks and jeeps," Stacy responded, "and often times on foot. Marti told me all about it."

"I always thought it was nuts to do what they do." Luke blurted out. "You've got all these brilliant archeologists from major universities all over the world, hacking their way through the mountain jungles with a machete, trying the whole time to keep their jeeps from being stuck in the mud while fighting off giant mosquitos and watching for snakes at every step."

"Well, I can't wait for him to get home so we can find out more about the ink." Stacy said. "

I'd sure like to know what they put in that stuff to make the colors so intense." Luke added.

"I know. I've never seen anything like it." Stacy agreed.

Luke leaned back in his chair and wondered out loud, "Can you imagine what people would say if these Mayan tattoos started showing up here in Miami?"

"Our business would explode." Stacy said with dollar signs in her eyes. "Everybody will want one. We could even sell the ink."

"We'd make a fortune." Luke agreed.

"Maybe we could take care of our problem." Stacy offered.

"I'm sorry Stacy." Luke said. "It's my fault we're in this situation."

"It's ok baby, you know how much I love you. We'll get through this." She replied.

That night, as they lay in bed staring at the ceiling, they resigned themselves to the fact that there was nothing they could do except wait for her Uncle to return. So they decided to put the ink out of their minds for now - *but that was easier said than done.*

Early the next day, Jack Jennings walked into Luke's tattoo shop looking for a consult.

"Hi, I'm Jack," he said, and reached out to shake Luke's hand. But before he could respond, the customer he had been working on sat up grinning from ear to ear.

"Hi, it's nice to meet you. I'm Bob, and I'm a huge fan." he said. Then he looked up at Luke and asked "Do you know who this is?"

"Yes" Luke admitted as he turned to shake Jack's hand, "everybody in Miami knows Jack Jennings."

Two guys that looked like cops had come in with Jack. They were polite. They smiled and nodded at Luke but didn't introduce themselves or speak at all the whole time they were there.

"Did you see the game?" Bob asked.

"Unfortunately, yes. I lost a lot of money on that game." Luke lamented.

"A lot of other people did too." Bob said. "Who would have thought that Jack would get hurt and have to leave the game in the first five minutes?"

"Nobody's more disappointed than I am fellows" Jack said. "This type of injury, where the tendons are completely worn away from the bone is serious."

Luke shook his head and added, "I turned the game off at halftime. The Dolphins were down by three touchdowns and it was getting ugly. I couldn't watch it anymore."

"You didn't miss much." Jack continued. "It was all downhill from there." It was the worst loss of my life, but if I can get this broken arm to cooperate, I'll get back on the field and redeem myself."

"After the career you've had, it would be a shame to see you go out this way. But you can be sure of one thing, the fans still love you." Bob said.

Jack looked at Bob and smiled. "My father always taught me to appreciate the fans. They're the ones that make football great. And here in Miami, our fans have always been our secret weapon."

He shook Bob's hand and gave him an autograph plus a selfie. Bob was as happy as a kid at Christmas. Then Jack looked back at Luke and continued speaking, and as he did, he pulled a folded piece of paper out of his pocket.

"I've heard good things about your work, Luke. I've got a design here for a tattoo to commemorate our AFC

Championship win. I'd like you to take a look at it, but since you're busy I'll come back later. What does your schedule look like for tomorrow?" Jack asked.

"No, no; wait." Bob said. "I don't mind waiting while you guys go over this." So Jack spread the paper with the tattoo drawing out over the counter and proceeded to review each piece, being careful to explain the significance of various symbols in the design. Afterwards, Jack made an appointment to get the work done.

As he was leaving, Luke acted on an impulse and stopped him.

"Wait," he said as he reached under the counter and pulled out the pictures Stacy's Uncle had sent. "I've got something I want to show you guys."

As Jack looked at the pictures, a puzzled look came over his face. "These the most beautiful tattoo I've ever seen." he said.

"I know, my wife and I both said the same thing."

"Where did you get these?" Bob asked.

"My wife's Uncle sent it to us from Honduras," Luke said. "He's at the Mayan ruins in Copan. These are pictures of Mayan villagers who live in the mountain near there. He thought the tattoos were extraordinary and wanted us to see them. They also found wall carvings about a special tattoo ink that gives the wearer superhuman abilities."

"Where did they get that ink?" Jack wanted to know.

"We don't know. There was a partial formula on a wall carving at one of the temple in Copan."

"How can we get some?" Jack asked.

19

"Stacy's Uncle thinks the tattoo's you're looking at may have been done with that same ink. He's trying to finish the translation, and hopefully, he'll have the rest of the formula by the time he gets home."

"When's he coming home?" Jack wanted to know.

"We don't have the exact date, but it'll be some time in the next six or eight weeks."

Jack was momentarily silent, and then he got an impatient look on his face.

"We have to get this ink for my new tattoo, and I don't want to wait six or eight weeks to get it. Maybe we can find somebody down there who knows something about it."

"That's what I was thinking Jack. I did a search on the internet this morning for tattoo artists in Honduras. I found a couple, and made several calls, but these guys are hard to get ahold of. I did speak to a few of them."

"The first guy didn't speak English very well, and all I could get out of him was that a Shaman did it. The second guy didn't speak English at all. And the third guy said it was a religious thing, and told me to mind my own business" Luke continued.

"It sounds like he knows something," Jack said.

"That's what I thought too." Luke agreed. "But he also told me there was a Curse that would befall anyone who tried to use the ink except a Mayan Shaman."

"What's a Shaman?" Bob asked.

"He's a Holy Man, kind of like a High Priest." Luke responded.

Jack got a sarcastic look on his face and remarked "Well fortunately, I don't believe in all that hocus pocus stuff." Then he thought about it for a second and his eyes lit up. "I know what we're going to do. We'll go down there and pay off anybody that'll sell us some of that ink. Do you have a passport?"

"Sure," Luke said, "but my wife Stacy is pregnant."

"Congratulations." Jack said.

"Thanks, but I think she's too far along for a trip like that, and I wouldn't want to leave her alone in her condition. But it sounds tempting. Stacy's Uncle told us that the scenery is breathtaking and the ruins are incredible."

"Well, my wife Mary was a nurse before we got married. We'll take her down there with us."

"I don't know." Luke said. "I'll ask Stacy and see what she thinks. I do know her well enough to know that she would love to go on a trip like this if her Doctor will give her the go ahead."

"Ok then, we'll go down there for a week or so until we find that ink. We'll take Stacy and my wife Mary with us. It'll be a blast. Close the shop for a week, and I'll pay you whatever it takes to get you down there. Maybe we'll even do the tattoo while we're there."

"It sounds wonderful Jack, but honestly, I can't leave Miami," Luke said. "Although I'll have to admit I'm tempted. If I could get my hands on some of that ink, it would change a lot of things around here and solve a lot of problems."

"What kind of problems?" Jack said.

"Well actually, this is kind of your fault. I bet big on the Dolphins to win the Super Bowl. Everybody said you would win. It was a foregone conclusion. So I took the inheritance money my aunt left me and put it all on Miami to win. The problem is, my inheritance money has gotten held up in probate, and I can't get my hands on any of it. Now my bookie's men have been pressing me for the money I lost, but there's no way I can come up with that kind of cash until the inheritance arrives. Unfortunately, I don't think Tico's going to wait that long, and Stacy and I are worried. I need to pay off this gambling debt before something bad happens."

"This could be just the ticket." Jack said.

"You could become a celebrity." Bob chirped in. "Maybe even a TV show about tattoos."

"Ok Jack. I'll talk to Stacy tonight and see what she thinks."

"Great. I'm having a barbecue on Saturday. Why don't you guys come over and we can talk about it then?"

"Ok, I'll double check with Stacy, but that should be good."

Jack wrote down his address and gave it to Luke. When he left, the first thing he did was call Stacy.

"Hi, where are you?"

"Hi. I'm grocery shopping" she said.

"Guess who was in my shop just now."

"I don't know. Tell me."

"Jack Jennings."

"Do you mean Jack Jennings from the Miami Dolphins?"

"Yeah, and he invited us to a barbecue at his house this weekend," Luke said.

"Are you serious?"

"Yeah I'm serious." He continued.

"That sounds like fun." Stacy replied. "Maybe we'll meet some celebrities."

"I wouldn't be surprised, but there's something else. Jack wants to go to Honduras to look for some of that tattoo ink, and he wants us to go with him. He says he'll cover all of our expenses and pay me whatever it takes to get us down there."

"Oh Luke, maybe we can get enough to pay Tico before you get hurt."

"Yeah, that's what I was thinking. If we can come home with some of that ink, it could save us."

"It sounds exciting Luke. We need the money, and I could visit Uncle Robert. But how long would we be gone?"

"I don't know, but I'm guessing we'd be gone about a week or so. I don't want you to be away from your doctor for too long or take any unnecessary chances with the babies."

"I agree." Stacy said. "I can go back to see Dr. Parker again tomorrow."

"Yes. Let's find out what he thinks before we commit to anything." Luke agreed.

"Ok." Stacy said.

"When are you coming home?" Luke asked.

"I'm just finishing up now, so I should be home in about hour or so."

"Ok, I'll see you when I get there."

After Bob left, Luke began closing down the shop. He was in the back when he heard the bell chime. Someone was out front, but when I came around to the front of the shop he stopped short in his tracks. He recognized the two thugs that were waiting for him. They worked for his bookie, Jose "Tico" Morales.

"Mr. Taylor, we missed you today." One of the thugs said.

"I know. The money didn't come today, but as soon as it does I swear you'll be my first stop."

"Well now, that may be a problem. Tico is not a patient man, and he doesn't understand excuses."

"Tell him he'll get his money."

"Oh yes, he knows he will. Tico told me to cut off one of your fingers every time we come by and you don't have the money" the thug said as he as he grabbed Luke by the collar and lifted him off the ground. He produced a knife with a six inch blade from his inside jacket pocket, then he grabbed Luke's hand and forced it onto the countertop where he positioned the knife in a good place to take off one of his fingers.

"Of course, the problem with that is that you need your hand to make money. So Tico said to give you one more week." the thug said as he finally released him.

The other thug who was with him had been silent up to this point. But as they turned around to leave, he reached into his pocket and produced a knife as well. He reached over and stuck the knife into one of Luke's tattoo tables and opened it up from one end to the other. Then he smiled and they both laughed as they left.

The next day, Stacy and Luke visited her doctor, and as they sat in the waiting room, they debated the pros and cons of going to Honduras.

"I wonder what Dr. Parker's going to say about this." Luke said.

"I don't know," Stacy said as she squeezed Luke's hand. "I want to go, but not if it won't be safe."

"I want to go too" Luke agreed

. "If we could get some of that ink we might be able sell it and pay off Tico before he starts cutting off my fingers."

"What's the latest on your inheritance?" Stacy asked.

"They have a buyer for the house, but they're waiting for the loan to close before they divide up the rest of the money. I swear Stacy, I really thought the money would be here by now. I thought I could bet on a sure thing and win enough for us to pay off the tattoo shop."

"I know Baby." Stacy said. "This trip could save us if I

can get Dr. Parker to give me the go ahead."

And he did exactly that.

Stacy's doctor surprised them. He gave her a long list of do's and don'ts for the trip, but cleared her to go since she was only going to be gone for a week or two at the most. So with the Doctor's approval in hand, they agreed that they would go to Jack's barbeque to see what he had in mind.

When Saturday finally arrived they went to the barbecue, and when they got there, Jack's place was rocking.

They pulled up to the house and the valet greeted them at the front door. He held the car door for Stacy, and gave Luke a claim ticket for their vehicle.

As they walked away Luke looked at his wife and chuckled under his breath, "I wondered what the valet must have thought of our car after parking Bentley's and Porches all night."

"I don't know" said Stacy, "but it gets twenty-five miles per gallon in the city," and they both laughed, but when they stepped inside they quit laughing.

Stacy was wide-eyed and whispered in Luke's ear, "This place is unbelievable."

"Yeah, I know." he agreed. "It's bigger than I ever

imagined a house could be."

"Calling this place a house is like calling the Vatican a chapel." Stacy quipped. "It's an estate."

"Yeah, and I heard this property has its own private beach." Luke added.

They made their way through the massive foyer and out the glass doors into the pool area, which looked like an exclusive Caribbean resort, with a swim-up bar and a giant Miami Dolphins logo at the bottom of the pool. The whole area was lit up with torches and soft lighting, and music was booming through the sound system.

They strolled around the pool area until they spotted Jack out by the grill; which was actually a giant barbecue pit behind the pool overlooking the ocean. There were a half-dozen guys hanging around, drinking beer, and watching the steaks sizzle. Jack was at the controls, and when he spotted Luke he motioned them over.

"Luke, I'm glad you could make it."

"Hi Jack. Thanks for inviting us."

"And this must be Stacy. Luke told me all about you."

"It's nice to meet you Jack."

Stacy noticed that Jack's arm was still in a soft cast and inquired about it.

"Does it hurt?"

"Not too bad." Jack replied. "But I sure am tired of wearing this cast on my arm."

"I can imagine." Luke said.

There was a man telling jokes to the guys hanging around the grill. Jack got his attention and motioned him over. "Max, there's somebody I'd like you to meet."

Jack reached out and put his arm around Max as he joined them.

"Max, let me introduce you to Luke. He's the one who's going to do my new tattoo."

Max reached out to shake Luke's hand, then looked over at Stacy.

"And who is this lovely lady?"

"Hi, I'm Stacy. It's nice to meet you."

"Max is my Agent, my Business Manager, and my best friend" Jack said. We go all the way back to the days when we played football together for the Fighting Irish. Max was the best damn running back to ever wear a Notre Dame uniform."

"Ok Jack, that's enough," Max said.

"He's modest, but he was a force of nature."

Jack turned his attention back to the grill while Max went back to cracking jokes with the guys.

"Hey Max, after you guys won the AFC Title Game, I heard the other team had some trouble at the airport." One of the men joked.

"Oh Yeah," Max said. "They missed their plane because somebody painted the terminal to look like the end zone and they couldn't find it."

He was hilarious, and had the whole group howling.

"You know, Max is a classic American success story," Jack said. "He was a poor kid from Detroit who grew up in the ghetto. But he was smart and stayed away from the whole drug and gang scene. Instead, he spent his afternoons in the weight room and focused on football. He was a high school All-American, and won a full scholarship to play football at Notre Dame."

Shortly after Jack said that, Max walked back over and spoke to him quietly. "That security issue we discussed has been taken care of."

"Good." Jack said, as he went back to grilling the steaks.

Max excused himself and headed towards the house. As he walked away, Luke noticed he walked with a limp, and asked Jack about it.

"That's an old football injury. Max got hurt saving my ass," Jack said. "One of these days I'll break out some of the old Notre Dame game films. His running was pure poetry in motion."

When Jack spoke about Max, Luke could see the pain in his eyes. *"I guess he never forgave himself for what happened to Max"* he thought.

"You know, Luke," Jack continued, "I'm thirty-three years old. In NFL years I'm ancient. The Dolphins continue to start me because I win. Age is just a number, and I'm playing the best football of my life. Right now I'm at the top of my game. But that could change."

"What's the prognosis on your arm?" Luke asked.

"They don't know. In the meantime, there are four young quarterbacks in the clubhouse with shotgun arms who are competing for my job. And the best man starts. No exceptions. So if I'm going to continue to quarterback this team, I better make sure my arm is one-hundred percent. That's why I was intrigued by the part of the inscription that referred to superhuman abilities. If there is some kind of healing agents buried in the rainforest, I want to know about it. And at the very least, we'll come away with a beautiful tattoo. So, are you guys ready to go to Honduras?"

"Yes" Luke said. "We're looking forward to getting our hands on some of that ink too. Have you worked out any details?"

"Max handles all that stuff for me, and he's already working on it," Jack said.

Just then a woman approached us. She was unusually beautiful, and although she was wearing a loose-fitting silk gown, anyone could see that she was in fantastic shape. When Jack spotted her, he smiled and his eyes lit up.

"Let me introduce you to my wife, Mary".

"Mary, there's somebody I'd like you to meet" he said. "This is Luke Taylor and his wife Stacy. There're the ones who found out about the tattoo ink, and they're coming with us to Honduras."

"That's great. I'm Mary" she said. "It's nice to meet you two. I haven't seen the pictures yet, but Jack is really excited about this tattoo ink."

"We are too," Stacy echoed. "But because of my condition we can't stay for more than a week or so."

"How far along are you?" Mary asked a she admired Stacy's baby bump.

"Almost seven months. But my doctor has cleared me to go, and I'm really excited about the trip."

"Well, we'll have plenty of time to get to know each other. I've never been to Central America, but I understand it's beautiful. I thought I heard Jack say you have an Uncle down there?"

"Yes. He's an archeologist, and he's the one who sent us the pictures."

"I'm looking forward to meeting him" Mary said. Then she excused herself to attend to her other guests.

When the food was ready, the waiters started serving dinner. Their guests sat under a covered patio, enjoying the food as they listened to the roar of the ocean. There was a cool breeze gently blowing through the palm trees, and Stacy and Luke were overwhelmed by the whole experience.

After dinner, they milled about for another hour or so. But the food and drink, combined with all the excitement about the trip finally caught up with them. They found Jack out by the pool bar and thanked him for inviting them.

"Thanks for having us over Jack. Stacy and I had a great time."

"It was my pleasure; and it was nice to meet you Stacy as well. Max will take care of all the details, and he'll get in touch with you. We'd like to leave as soon as possible. How soon could you be ready?"

"I think we can rearrange our schedules and be freed up in a couple of days."

"That's perfect. Max will get in touch with you and go

over everything."

"That'll be great Jack; we're looking forward to going. But for me to close the shop down for a week is going to be expensive. We never discussed my fee."

"What's fair? Jack said."

"Well, I have a pressing financial matter, so if I'm going to close down the shop for a whole week, we're talking about ten grand." Luke said.

Jack paused momentarily, and you could see the wheels turning in his head. He looked at Luke and made him a proposition.

"I'll give you the ten thousand now, before we leave. If we find the ink, I'll double it and give you another ten."

Stacy and Luke looked at each other and tried not to act too excited. This would take care of Tico and they'd still have money left over, so they agreed to it.

They thanked Jack again, found their way back to the valet station, and left.

On the drive home, they recounted the events of the evening. They had never experienced a party like that one, and their heads were spinning. They just had a close-up look at life in the fast lane, and it was exhilarating. What they didn't realize was that the road they had started down was going to take them to a place beyond their wildest imaginations.

Chapter 3

As the plane banked to make its final approach, Luke got his first look at Honduras from the cabin window. The city below was a carousel of lights nestled in a blanket of mountains.

"Baby, are you still asleep?" He whispered.

"No, just resting." she said, still half-asleep with her eyes closed and her head resting on his shoulder. She looked out the window just in time to get a quick peek before the plane banked again. Then she looked into his eyes, smiled, and laid her head back on his shoulder.

As the plane touched ground in San Pedro Sula, Luke looked at his watch. It was ten o'clock at night. They had been traveling for over sixteen hours. They had to change planes twice: once in Houston, and again in Mexico City. They were exhausted.

The plane taxied to the terminal and they waited until it was secured. Once they were given permission to disembark, they made their way to the door. As they stepped out of the plane, Luke realized that they would have to descend stairs that led directly to the tarmac. He turned to help Stacy with one hand, and wrestled their carry-on luggage with the other, while also trying not to lose his grip on the railing.

"Are you okay honey?" He was asking her, while murmuring under my breath *"What the hell are we doing here?"*

He followed the crowd that led them through the night air. As they approached the door, Luke scanned the inside of the terminal for a familiar face. All he could see was an ocean of strangers and he momentarily froze. Fortunately, as he and Stacy stepped through the door, Max was there to greet them.

"You made it. How was your trip?"

"It was exhausting." Stacy said. "I'm ready for a nice hot bath and a soft bed."

"Well, we've got a nice room all ready for you at the hotel." Max assured her; then he looked back at Luke and said "Give me your baggage claim tickets and let's get you two out of here." He said something to one of the men who were with him, then looked back at Stacy and whimsically spoofed, "Madam, your carriage awaits."

They were whisked through the terminal by the security team and ushered into the back of a dark blue Suburban with blacked-out windows. As they pulled away from the curb, Luke noticed that the lead car they were following had four guards. There were another two in the Suburban with them, and they were all armed to the teeth.

Back home, Jack was normally accompanied by a security detail. Stacy and Luke met several of Jack's security team in the Tattoo Shop at the Bar-B-Que. He was an international celebrity, recognized all over the world. He was also Miami's favorite son, mobbed by well-wishing fans everywhere he went. All that enthusiasm and affection can make it difficult to get around; so purely as a practical matter, he normally utilized a low visibility security detail in public. But the security personnel that normally accompanied Jack back home looked like ex-military, or possibly secret service; and Jack insisted that his security team never display a weapon in public.

That was until tonight.

These guys were packing serious heat and weren't making any effort to camouflage it. In fact, it was just the opposite. They carried what looked to Luke like automatic rifles. In addition, they each carried several other weapons strapped to their bodies; and wore bullet proof vests in an obvious effort to deter potential threats. These men looked more like mercenaries.

"So, I bet you guys are hungry?" Max nervously remarked as he tried to play down the obvious concern he saw on their faces. Then he added, "Hey, we're not in Kansas anymore."

"I can see that, but why is all this necessary?" Luke asked.

"Jack wanted to be sure your trip was uneventful. This is something we have to deal with everywhere we go," Max shrugged, trying to downplay the situation.

They traveled down 7 Calle SO until they reached 13 Avenita SO. They turned left and headed towards the highway, but were soon stopped when traffic came to a complete halt. Up ahead they could see a Police roadblock, and traffic was being carefully routed around the quarantined area.

As they approached the scene, the security team in the first car spoke with the police, who cleared them to pass. The lead car called back to let the others know that they were passing the remnants of a botched kidnapping attempt. As they drove past the carnage, Luke could make out the bodies of several dead men inside a still smoking Ford van.

The van windows were dark, but he could clearly see four dead bodies. Stacy gasped and turned away, but Luke couldn't help looking. They were covered in blood, each laying in a different contorted pose, shot in the midst of a gun battle with the police. One man's head was partially blown off and his brains were exposed. Another had been shot in the chest several times, and his hand was partially shot off. It was a gruesome sight, and it was the first time Luke had ever seen anyone dead outside of a funeral home. It shook him to his core.

"How far is it to the hotel?" Stacy wondered out loud. "Where are we staying"?

"We've got you at the Hilton Princess," said Max.

"Look," Stacy blurted out. "They've got McDonalds," as we passed a building with the Golden Arches on the roof. It lit up the night sky like a monument to American pop culture in the midst of this foreign land. Soon they began to notice other familiar signs. Some had logos which they recognized, but with the words in Spanish.

In many ways San Pedro Sula looks like Miami with one key difference. While Miami is a city that is sometimes embattled in drug and crime issues, San Pedro Sula is a war zone. It's the murder capital of the world, and the most dangerous city in Honduras. Every building they passed in that part of the city was in complete lockdown. They all had steel bars covering the windows and doors, which obviously wasn't enough to keep out the criminal element, because many businesses were also protected by eight feet of metal fence topped by another two feet of razor wire.

"Max, how much further is it?" Stacy asked as she stretched. "My back is really hurting."

"Not far. You're almost home."

Max continued to make small talk as they rolled past block after block of urban battlefield. He tried to play down their concerns with platitudes about the food and the attractions in San Pedro Sula and at the ruins in Copan.

The lead car and the Suburban had stopped for a light. When they did, two older teenage boys started to cross the street. They stopped directly in between the two vehicles. One of the two boys looked the driver of the Suburban directly in the eye, then raised a pistol and pointed it at his head.

"What the hell is going on up there?" Max demanded.

"This territory belongs to one of the gangs that rule this area and this is a toll road." said one of the security guards. "Anytime you want to pass through this gang's territory, you're going to have to pay a toll."

"Is that what they're doing now?" Luke asked.

"No, Senor" said the Security Guard. "You are under the protection of Juan Rodriguez, so as far as the gangs are concerned, you are untouchable.

Luke was sitting in a good spot to see what was going on. One of the Security Guards from the first car got out to confront the gang members. He spoke with them for a few minutes, and then turned around and got back into the lead car.

"It looks like he's getting back in the car and they are letting us pass." Luke said. "Does this kind of thing happen all the time down here?"

"Unfortunately, San Pedro Sula is a very dangerous place." Max said. "But no need to worry. Once you get to the hotel you'll feel right at home."

As they moved into the heart of downtown, the scenery gradually changed. The gang graffiti was replaced by American Express and Visa logos. Soon the steel bars and barbed wire began to dissipate, and they found themselves in a modern commercial city of glass and steel.

Pedestrians briskly walked the sidewalk, block after block, despite the late hour. Shops were open, and customers lined up at the street food that was in plentiful supply.

"San Pedro Sula is a city that never sleeps" Max remarked.

They finally reached the Hilton and pulled up to the valet station. The facility was first rate, and the staff was crisp and professional. The valet unloaded their baggage, and guided them into the lobby.

Inside the hotel, Stacy and Luke were overwhelmed with what they saw. The place was an architectural work of art. The lobby was expansive, with floors made from Italian marble, and a dramatically curved white wooden staircase which dominated the room and connected the first and second floors. The staircase and the entire second floor were flanked by an ornate brass handrail, so brightly polished it appeared to be made of gold.

Jack and Mary had arrived the day before, and someone must have let them know that Luke and Stacy were there because they came down to greet them almost immediately. Mary ran over to Stacy and gave her a big hug. Jack crossed the distance from the elevators to where we were standing in about five steps, and when he saw them, his face lit up.

"Luke. Stacy. You made it," he exclaimed.

"Hi Jack," Stacy replied with a smile, holding her aching back with one hand and holding onto Luke for support with the other.

"Oh my, look at you," said Jack. "I bet you're beat."

"Well," Stacy started to explain, but before she could finish the thought Jack interrupted her.

"No, no, no. Let's get you off your feet." And with that he and Mary ushered them towards the elevators and personally walked them to their room. The whole time, Jack would point out pieces of Mayan artwork displayed in the hotel, and wax eloquently about the mysteries of the ancient Mayan war cults.

Stacy was wide-eyed. She had the innate sensibility to recognize the spiritual connections between Mayan art, culture, and religion. And like Luke, she had never been out of the country except for their Jamaican honeymoon. They certainly never expected to get to see the Mayan ruins at Copan firsthand, so they were both a little wide-eyed.

"Why don't I let you guys get settled," Jack offered.

"I'm sure you can use some rest."

"Ok," Stacy smiled.

As Jack turned to leave, he leaned into Luke and whispered "I'll be downstairs in the bar for a while. Try to make it down before you turn in." Then he smiled back at Stacy and closed the door behind himself as he and Mary left.

"Whew!" they sighed in unison.

Stacy fell onto the bed and began moaning, "Oh… this bed feels so good."

"Oh, yeah," Luke agreed, as he fell onto the couch.

They were hungry, so they ordered room service. While we waited for the food to be brought up, Stacy slipped into a hot bath and they talked.

"You know, I'm going to have to go down there," Luke said as he stood by the sink and splashed cold water on his face.

"Go down where, to the bar?"

"Yes. He obviously wants to talk about something."

He knew she would understand. He was exhausted, but by now their curiosity was aroused, and he couldn't sleep if he tried. So after the food arrived and Stacy was settled in bed, Luke kissed her goodnight and went downstairs looking for Jack.

As the elevator made its way from the eighth floor to the lobby, Luke felt a growing sense of impatience. He'd come a long way because Jack had asked him to, and now that he was here, he was more determined than ever not to leave without ink.

When he reached the ground floor he looked at his watch as the doors were opening. It was 11:30pm. He stepped into the lobby, rounded the corner, and followed the hallway that led to Clancy's Bar.

San Pedro Sula is a major commercial center. Business travelers from all over the world frequent the city, and historically there has always been a heavy contingency of British visitors. Many of them stay at the Hilton, and when they do, they feel right at home at Clancy's.

It's a traditional English-style pub. The walls, ceiling, and windows are made of rich Mahogany with ornate carvings, and the room is filled with overstuffed chairs centered in small groups around circular wooden tables with large glass ashtrays.

Luke opened one of the two heavy wooden doors at the entrance and coughed as he stepped into a cloud of cigar smoke. Scanning the room, he spotted Jack and Max at a table in the corner by the fireplace. Jack noticed him and motioned him over. Max stood up and guided Luke into his chair while signaling the waiter to bring another round.

"Did you guys get something to eat" Jack asked.

"Yes, thank you, we ordered room service."

Luke glanced around the room to get his bearings. There were about twenty people in a room that could easily seat a sixty. The place was dimly lit, except for the lights coming from the bar and the fireplace. He noticed a man sitting in the corner, near the bar, who appeared to be a security guard.

Finally, Luke turned to Jack and asked "Why such

heavy security measures? Since we got here, we've seen security guards everywhere."

"Honduras is a dangerous place," Jack said, "and San Pedro Sula is ground zero."

"He's not kidding," Max continued. "Eighty percent of the cocaine consumed in the United States passes through this city."

"How do you know all this?" Luke asked.

"I always do my homework before we take one of these trips." Max said. "The drugs come up from Colombia by boat. Once the drugs come ashore, there are literally thousands of miles of unpatrolled mountain roads."

"It's a distribution system that even FedEx would envy" Jack added.

"It's true," Max agreed with a shrug and a measure of admiration for the pure simplicity and bravado with which the drug lords run their operation. "You've got to take your hat off to these guys. Everybody on both sides of the border knows what they're doing; but nobody can stop it."

"And in Honduras, all roads lead to San Pedro Sula," Jack added. "It's a major transportation hub, because of the mountains; and there's no good way to get through this country without going through here."

"Yeah, this place is busy, and the gangs get a piece of everything," Max continued. "When I was doing the advance work for this trip, I found out there are two gangs that run this town. Their leaders demand tribute every week from every business operating in the city; every taxi, every restaurant, every hotel, every bar, and even the old man selling tamales out of a cart on the street corner. Everybody pays both gangs every week no matter what. You pay or you die. So, I hired a local company to provide security."

"They also provide protection from ambitious independents," Jack added.

"What do you mean by *ambitious independents*?" Luke questioned.

"Apparently, they have a thriving kidnapping industry in this country," Jack said. And as they continued drinking, he explained how it works.

"Unlucky members of wealthy families in the city are regularly abducted at gun point in broad daylight. They are normally roughed up a little, held in seclusion up in the mountains for a couple of weeks, and then released after the abductors were confident they had squeezed all they could from the victim's worried family. It's quite a racket."

"Well, if it's safe to leave the table, I'm going to the bathroom." Luke said.

He stood up and made his way towards the restroom. As he did he passed two middle-aged men who were sitting at the bar drinking heavily. They were drunk and began to get louder as they spouted a diatribe of insults at the British government and the Queen.

The bartender, who was very British, was getting angry. The insults offended him, but he kept his cool. However, he refused to serve the belligerent customers any more alcohol because they were already past the limit. From there, things got ugly.

"What do you mean we can't have another drink?"

"Why don't I have someone help you fellows to your

rooms? You look like you could use a good night's sleep" the bartender offered, trying to calm his drunken customers.

"Why don't I punch you in the mouth? You look like you could use to have your ass kicked" the taller man said.

About that time the security guard stepped in, but the drunks were not intimidated.

"Hey there mate, calm down. The bartender's right, you guys have had enough. Why don't I call someone to help you?"

"Why don't you shut up?" the other man said right before he picked up a heavy glass ashtray and smashed it into the security guards face. The bartender, who by now was livid, ran out from behind the bar to help the security guard who was on the ground bleeding profusely.

Just at that moment, Luke was walking back to his table from the bathroom and accidently stepped right into the middle of the fight.

The Security Guard was still down, and the bartender who had rushed to his aid was now lying on the ground as the two drunks stood over them, kicking and beating them to a pulp. In the meantime, the few customers who were left in the bar stood and watched in silence, but nobody raised a finger to help.

Luke came up behind the taller man, grabbed him by the collar, and threw him to the ground. The other drunk took a swing at him, but Luke dodged the punch and then counter punched the guy in the mouth. The drunk grabbed his face in pain, and then stepped back up to take another swing, but Luke saw it coming. He threw hard punch at the drunk and knocked the guy completely off his feet. He stood over the man and waited to see if he was down or if he was getting back up; but he wasn't moving. Then, without warning, the taller man picked himself up off the floor and sucker punched Luke in the back of the head, knocking him into the bar. But before the man had a chance to hit Luke again, Max was there and waded into the guy with a barrage of punches and kicks that ended the fight quickly. When it was over; the Security Guard, the bartender, and the two drunks were all laid out on the barroom floor.

Luke looked over at Max with a sense of awe. "Where did you learn to fight like that?"

"What can I tell you man? I grew up in Detroit." Max said.

The Police arrived soon after that. They sent the Security Guard and the Bartender to the hospital in an ambulance. The two drunks were taken straight to jail. After that they closed the bar, so the three of them went up to Max's room for one more drink.

"I saw one of those tattoos on an old man at the airport" Jack said. "Only the colors on the old man were even more beautiful than the one's I had seen on the younger men in the pictures Stacy's uncle sent you. I kept trying to ask him where he got that tattoo, but all he would tell me is that the Shaman did it. And I agree with Luke, I think this is a religious thing. So early tomorrow, we'll head up to Copan. Once we get the girls settled we can go up into the mountains and find a Shaman, but we're going to need a guide."

"Stacy and I already thought about that, so she wrote her Uncle a letter before we left. Hopefully it gets to him before we do."

"And hopefully we can get a guide who can help us

find the ink." Jack said.

They continued talking and drinking for another thirty-minutes, but Luke was only halfway paying attention. He had consumed too much alcohol and was too tired from the events of the day to focus, so he excused himself and went back to his room.

When he got there Stacy was asleep, so he washed up and got into bed without disturbing her. And as he lay beside her in the dark, listening to her softly breathing, he kept asking himself the same question over and over again – *"Why did I bring my pregnant wife to this dangerous place? "*

"Stacy, what time is it?" Luke asked as he pulled the covers over his head. He was trying to ignore the morning sun that was bursting through the cracks around the edges of the window, but it wasn't working. He momentarily forgot they were in Honduras, and glanced at the alarm clock to get his bearings. It read 7:45am, but it felt later. He was still worn out from the long trip yesterday.

"Are you up?" Stacy called from the bathroom. "We told Jack and Mary that we'd be ready to go by 9:00am and we don't want to keep them waiting."

"Ok, I'm getting up" Luke said as he dragged himself out of bed, stumbled towards the bathroom and turned on the hot water.

"I'm going to take a quick shower," he said, "and then I'll pack up our stuff."

"Great. I've already called room service to bring breakfast up. They should be here soon."

"Have you spoken with your Uncle Robert?" He called out from the shower.

"Yes, he's back at the base camp, and he said he will meet us tonight in Copan. He said he has a guide for us."

"That's great. Will you please pass me a towel?"

"Here you go." She said as she handed it to him.

He jumped out of the shower and got ready to leave in record time. He gulped down breakfast, finished packing up their stuff, and called for the baggage to be carried downstairs.

They all met in the lobby at nine. The air was electric, and everyone was bursting with anticipation as they loaded their luggage and climbed into the back of the Suburban. There were four security guards traveling with them, two in the Suburban, and two in the front car, all armed.

As they made their way through the city, Luke noticed Honduran army personnel standing guard at bus stops to protect citizens boarding and leaving the bus, and he wondered out loud how difficult it must be for the people who live there.

The farther they got from the Hilton, the more the scenery began to look like a war zone again. They continued another few miles, then headed West on CA 4. It's a major highway, and the only good way to get through the mountains to Copan. They traveled at a brisk pace for the first thirty minutes before traffic came to a complete stop.

"How long will it take to reach Copan?" Max asked one of the security guards.

"On a good day you can make in two and a half hours, but not today." He replied. "It'll probably take us every bit of four hours to get up there today."

"Why did the traffic just stop?" He continued. "Is there an accident?"

"Probably, it's not unusual up here." The guard said. "And once traffic finally does start moving again, we'll have an abundance of truck drivers determined to make up for lost time. It can be treacherous."

"But the scenery is so beautiful." said Mary.

"I know." said Jack. "Around every corner there's a breathtaking panoramic mountain view, and each one's more beautiful than the last. Look at the splashes of color from all the mountain foliage."

"And look at the birds." Stacy said. "There's almost an endless supply of macaws with the most beautiful brightly colored feathers I've ever seen."

"It almost makes you forget how treacherous this road is, doesn't it?" Luke said as he eyed the sharp drop offs on both sides of the truck.

"I almost can't look." Stacy said with a slight chill in her voice as she pondered the certain death that awaited them all if the driver was to take a wrong turn.

"Just close your eyes baby, we'll be there before you know it" Luke said as the truck continued to navigate the mountain roads for another three hours.

When they finally reached Copan they was stunned. It

felt like they were in a strange time warp. It was almost as if Mayans from ancient times have been transported into this small village in the shadow of the temple ruins.

The narrow streets of the city were lined on both sides with single story adobe buildings painted in a rainbow of jungle colors. The street itself was painted in some places with beautiful murals depicting a mixture of historical and religious images. They passed through an open market with stall after stall of merchants selling Mayan jewelry and artwork to the hundred and fifty or so tourists that pass through there each day. The air was filled with the sounds and smells of the market; and the driver slowed down and lowered the windows so they could take it all in. The smell of exotic food being cooked over open fires in the market, combined with the voices of the shopkeepers hawking their wares was intoxicating.

As they pulled up to the hotel, one of the guards turned around and gave them his best tourist pitch.

"The Hacienda San Lucas is a family run hotel, modern enough to get emails from Miami, and yet esthetically correct situated just a few hundred yards from the ruins. I'm certain that you have never seen anything like it" he assured them, and he was right.

As they checked in the concierge gave them a brief tour.

"From the dining area on the lawn behind the facility, there is an excellent view of the ruins, with stone temples rising out of the jungle over the tree tops." she said. "And in the kitchen, the women still make corn tortillas by hand and cook them over an open fire. All the food is made the traditional way," she boasted "with some recipes going back over a thousand years. And the waitresses still carry trays on their heads to your table."

"I would love to see that." said Mary.

"Well, why don't we all plan on meeting in the lobby at three o'clock so we can do the tour of the ruins, then meet for dinner at seven?" suggested Jack.

Everyone agreed, and they all went to their rooms to get settled.

At three o'clock they meet in the lobby and made the short walk to the ruins. They were all talking at once with anticipation when they rounded a section of the jungle trail and got their first look at Copan.

Tikal, the largest city in the classic Maya period, is often referred to as the New York of the Mayan universe. And if Tikal was New York, then Copan was Paris. Art and culture flourished like nowhere else. Stelas recounting the history and victories of great Mayan kings decorated the plaza, where majestic temples rise up to the sky. The ballfield sat in the center of the plaza, and was the site of many a ball game where the losers were put to death.

Stone paintings and cravings decorate the walls and were etched into the side of the monuments. Stairways rising to the top of the pyramid were engraved with the history of Copan, and a record of the kings who had ruled there.

Of particular interest to the group were the paint and dyes used to create the artwork. The colors were unbelievable, and looked like they had just been done yesterday, even though they were over a thousand years old.

Afterwards, the group retired to their rooms to prepare

for dinner.

The dinner party that night included Max, Jack, Mary, Stacy and Luke. The night air was pleasant, and the temperature seemed perfect. As the waitress was taking drink orders, a man and a woman approached the table. The security team had partitioned off a section of the dining area, but allowed them to pass after a few words. As they approached the table, Stacy recognized the man as her Uncle Robert. She jumped up from her seat and ran over to greet him with a big hug and a kiss on the cheek. Luke stood, smiled, and extended his hand.

"Uncle Robert, it's good to see you. We've missed you."

"Luke, it's so good to see you too." he replied. Stacy tells me that your tattoo shop is doing very well."

"Not too bad. How are you feeling these days?"

"I'm about the same. I have good days and bad days. The climate down here is not good for my arthritis. But this is such important work I can't let arthritis stop me, so we forge on."

Stacy introduced her Uncle to everyone at the table.

"I'd like you all to meet my Uncle, Dr. Robert Nolan. He's an Archeologist, and he's very intelligent." Stacy teased, much to her Uncle's dismay.

"You've been working down here for ... how long?" Luke asked.

"Five months now." He replied.

Stacy put her arm around her Uncle.

"My Uncle Robert is brilliant," she said, "and he has a big heart."

Luke could see that Uncle Robert was getting embarrassed so he leaped into the conversation.

"I don't think we've met your associate."

Neither Stacy nor Luke recognized the woman who was with him, but she was wearing a University of Miami polo shirt, so they assumed that she was part of the archeological team.

"It's nice to meet you all." Uncle Robert said. I'd also like to introduce Dr. Rosa Lazaro. She's from the University and has been working with us on the dig. She was one of my best graduate students at the University, and is going to be one of my best Associate Professors when we get home."

"Nice to meet you Rosa" Stacy replied, and then introduced everyone else at the table.

"Dr. Lazaro will be your guide tomorrow" Uncle Robert continued. "She herself is from a small village up in the mountains. Her family still lives up there, and they have arranged for you to meet a Shaman."

"Are you sure Rosa? We hate to take you away from your work," Jack said.

"Believe me, it will be my pleasure. I have been here

for five months, and this will only be the third time I have visited my parents, so I am overdue. We are a very close family, and I miss them."

"Why don't we sit down and order something to drink?" Max suggested as he motioned for Jack and Mary to move down a seat and held the chair next to his for Rosa.

"Dr. Lazaro, may I?"

"Well thank you Max," she said with a smile as they made eye contact and held it.

"Did you get a chance to tour the ruins yet?" she asked.

"Yes, after lunch this afternoon we took the tour and it was amazing" Stacy replied. "Luke and I were really fascinated with the art and sculptures.

"I was particularly fascinated with the colors." Luke said. "How is it that the colors look so good after being exposed to the elements for all this time?"

"That's part of the reason this place is considered sacred ground to Mayan people." Rosa said. And as they made their way through dinner, she told them the story of the great Mayan Prince Yax Mo', who led an army of warriors to this place, and founded a dynasty that ruled Copan for over four hundred years.

"I saw a picture of a macaw painted on the temple with a man's face coming out of its mouth," Stacy said, "and the colors were beautiful."

"I saw the same thing" Luke said. "But it was a snake with feathers."

"That is the Mark of the Feathered Serpent," Rosa said.

"He is a warrior and a healer. The tattoo is a mark of honor. When the Mayan Council of Elders senses the warrior is ready, he gets the Mark of the Feathered Serpent tattooed on the inside of his right forearm. The tattoos connect the warrior's spirit with the spirit of Kukulkan, the Mayan god of war. He empowers the warrior with the strength and speed of the jungle cats."

So you need a Shaman to do one of these tattoos?" Luke asked.

"Yes, a Shaman or a Master of Tattoo."

Stacy looked puzzled. "Do people still believe in that stuff?"

"Some people do," Rosa answered. "There are over seven million Mayan people living in the world, and a lot of them still believe in the old ways."

"What happened to all the people?" Jack said. "Why did everyone leave?"

"It was the drought. It was the worst drought in a thousand years. Here in Copan, they had over thirty-thousand people living in an area that would normally support about a third of that. They had a six-month rainy season, followed by six-months of drought. But because they were so advanced in mathematics, they were able to irrigate the land in such a way as to provide ample food. But when the drought came, the people were gradually forced to leave this place."

"They left to find food," Max concluded.

"Yes, to find food and to save their children."

"What do you mean *save their children*?" Mary

interjected.

"The Mayan people worship the rain god Chaac," Rosa continued. "And in times of severe drought, they would sacrifice young boys and girls."

"She's talking about the blue pit." Uncle Robert said.

"What do you mean *blue pit*?" Mary asked.

"They created a pit by burrowing out soft limestone. They collapsed the ceiling, and then allowed it to fill with rain water," Rosa said. "Here in Copan, there is a sixty-foot drop to the water below, followed by forty-feet of water, followed by ten-feet of mud, which is filled with human bones and precious articles thrown into the pit as a sacrifice to Chaac."

"Were the children thrown in alive?" Mary wanted to know.

"No, beside the pit there is a large rounded killing stone. The children were sacrificed at night, under a canopy of a thousand stars. They would be stretched across the top of the killing stone with eyes facing towards the night sky. The shaman would call out to Chaac to hear his prayer and accept this sacrifice. Then he plunged the ceremonial knife deep into the child's chest, cut out its still beating heart, and threw it into the pit along with the victim's corpse."

"What a horrible story," Mary said.

"Why is the water blue?" Luke wanted to know.

"It's the Mayan blue dye" said Rosa. "The children were all painted with Mayan Blue before they were sacrificed. It's a sacred dye made by the Shaman and it never fades. So even after the body has long ago decomposed in the pit, the dye looks as good in the water as it did the day they created it."

"Do you mean to tell me all that blue water we saw in that pit was really blue dye that came out of the bodies of decomposing children?" Mary fired back, obviously upset at the thought of that many sacrificed children.

"Yes," Rosa answered.

There was an awkward silence after she said that. Everyone at the table needed a minute to digest that information. Finally, Jack said, "Well, I'd like to find out more about the tattoo ink, and I'm looking forward to going up in the mountains tomorrow."

"We'll visit El Comino," Rosa said. "My father has arranged to have the Shaman come to our home, and then you can find out everything you want to know about the tattoos and the colors."

"Well I for one am looking forward to it," Max said "especially if Rosa is going to be our tour guide."

"It will be my pleasure," Rosa said as the waitress came back to the table for another round of drink orders.

After dinner, everyone sat and listened intently as Stacy's Uncle recounted stories of the great Mayan Kings and life in a Mayan village. The drinks were flowing and the weather was perfect. Time passed quickly, and eventually Stacy and Luke excused themselves and headed back to their room.

Luke went to bed restless that night. Stacy was looking forward to a couple of days of spa treatments at the hotel with Mary. He, on the other hand, had mixed feelings. He was certainly not thrilled with the idea of going that far into the jungle. Yet, his artistic soul was fascinated with the colors, and as he nodded off to sleep that night he kept thinking about an old Mayan saying I had heard.

"Don't invite a jaguar to dinner because you might end up on the menu."

Chapter 5

El Comino is a short day trip from Copan on Pan American Highway 11, which is a fancy name for a road that in some places is nothing more than one barely paved lane weaving through some of Central America's most rugged mountains. Around every curve is a sharp drop that would send the car careening to certain death. And yet, the unbridled beauty that surrounded them distracted everyone's attention from the perils of the journey.

When they left Copan that morning, two of the security guards stayed at the hotel with Stacy and Mary. The other two traveled in the Suburban with Luke, Jack, Max, and Rosa. After about two hours, they came to El Comino and turned onto a dirt street. It was several blocks long, containing a mixture of shops and residences. Some had doors and windows, and others were little more than open stalls. There were chickens wandering aimlessly through the street, as well as a dozen or so people. Some of them had horses or donkeys, and a few had cars. They pulled up in front of a brown two story building, and everyone stopped to look at them, than pretended to go back to what they were doing.

Rosa's family operated a small business on the first floor of the building and lived on the second. Her father had arranged to have the Shaman come to his home to meet with them, so he knew they were coming and met them on the porch.

Rosa's father was a charming man in his late fifty's with strong Latin features and a gentle voice. His fabric shop had everything from silk to burlap. And since the people who live in this area make most of their own cloths, Rosa's father had made a modest but comfortable living for many years.

He and Rosa hugged on the front porch and greeted one another in Spanish. After everyone was introduced they were led inside to the back of the store, then up a stairway to his family's private living quarters. It was sparse by American standards; but had the warm glow of a happy home. They were introduced to Rosa's mother, and her two sisters, and invited to join the family for dinner.

After an excellent dinner, Rosa led her guests out onto the covered patio, which wrapped around the whole building. Since there are so few two-story buildings in the town, it offered an excellent view of the surrounding area. It also offered Rosa's family a certain measure of protection.

As they sat on the porch enjoying the fine Cuban cigars Rosa brought for her father, it began to rain. Slowly at first, then at a steady pace until it was a complete downpour in less than a minute. The rain was so loud on the building's metal roof that talking became difficult, so they all sat silently smoking their cigars to the hypnotic rhythm of the rain.

As he sat there in silence, looking down the empty street, Luke spotted two men approaching from the end of the block. Just barely visible in the pouring rain, they weren't even trying to hurry or get out of the violent storm. He continued smoking under the covered patio as the two men continued to make their way towards them.

By the time they reached the house, Rosa's father recognized one of them as the Shaman and went down to greet him. When he did, they all came back in from the patio. Rosa's sisters had placed enough chairs in a circle to accommodate the entire party in anticipation of the Shaman's arrival. The lights were dimmed, and the room was lit by candle light. The girls placed incense burners around the room that produced the most beautiful aroma and a cloud of smoke that filled the air.

When the Shaman entered the room, everyone stood. He greeted the family first, and then the guests in turn. They all sat down and Rosa's sisters began serving Yage tea; first to the Shaman and his assistant, and then Jack, Max, and Luke, followed by the family.

Rosa had warned them about the tea.

"In Mayan culture, the use of hallucinogenic drugs is an essential aspect of our religion" said Rosa. "The Shamans make use of plants and roots to bring the faithful into an altered state in which they are able to communicate with God and bring back wisdom and knowledge, and the Yage tea is one of the most powerful brews."

"Is it safe?" Jack wanted to know.

"Yes, it is safe. It is traditionally used at festivals, and to honor visiting dignitaries. You are under no obligation to try the tea, but the Shaman is here to lead you into understanding." She also assured them that it would do them no harm, and that they would find what they were looking for. So, one by one, they all drank the tea.

Almost immediately Luke felt slightly drunk. Within a minute, he threw up; barely making it to the railing on the porch. As he leaned over the rail with his stomach in convulsions, he looked to his left to see Jack and Max doing the same. Eventually, he was able to make it back to his chair but was so dizzy he had to hold on to it to keep from falling out. He saw flashes of blue and purple light. The whole room seemed to hum and take on a glow, and he felt like he was sitting on a cloud.

His vision became razor sharp, and his mind opened. His thinking was crystal clear, and he suddenly understood many things. The Shaman sat directly across from him and gazed straight into his eyes. Luke was sure that the holy man was staring directly into his soul. Then he spoke to Luke in Mayan, and Rosa translated.

"You are seeking the ink."

"Yes, there's nothing like it in America. But we can't find anyone to help us. Everyone just keeps saying that a Shaman did it. Can you help us?"

"What would you do with the ink?" the Shaman asked, although he already knew the answer to the question.

"I would use it with my customers. The tattoos done with this ink are the most beautiful tattoos that any of us have ever seen. If I had this ink back in Miami, I could change the entire tattoo industry."

"You think the ink will help you accumulate wealth and power."

Jack interrupted the Shaman and said "I'd like to know more about the tattoo I saw that was a snake with feathers."

"What you refer is the Mark of the Feathered Serpent. When the Mayan Council of Elders agrees a warrior is ready, he gets the Mark of the Feathered Serpent tattooed on the inside of his right forearm. It is a mark of honor. It connects the Warrior's spirit with the spirit of Kukulkan, the god of war."

"My wife's Uncle has translated most of the formula for the ink from carvings on the Temple wall," Luke said, "but part of the formula is missing. It speaks of flowers from the jungle here in Copan, and clay; but it doesn't tell us how to actually prepare the ink. It also refers to another ingredient, but we can't make out what that ingredient is. If we had the missing piece of the formula, we could take some of the ingredients back to Miami and make the ink there."

"No. That will never happen." said the Shaman.

"Why?" Jack asked

"The tattoos are an open channel to the gods. The gods reach down from the heavens to touch the lives of their people. To use the power without the blessings of the gods is sacrilege, and anyone who receives the tattoo by anyone other than a Shaman or a Master of Tattoo will bring on the Curse."

What's the Curse?" Max asked.

"The Curse of the Feathered Serpent will befall anyone who tries to make his own tattoo." said the Shaman.

"Instead of enhancing the Warrior's strength, speed, and agility; it will cause him to lose his mind and there is no cure."

"Is there no one else who can do this tattoo?" Luke asked.

"No, only a Shaman or a Master of Tattoo can do the Mark of the Feathered Serpent. But we have many different tattoos. Some tattoos are for healing. Some are used to ward off spirits. Still others will bring the body and the mind of the tattooed into balance."

"Yes," conceded Rosa.

Then something happened. At first, Luke didn't know what it was. But as he sat there, the Shaman began to fall into a trance. His eyes were closed, and he was humming and chanting some sort of prayer in Mayan. Heaviness fell upon the room, and the air became so thick you could cut it with a knife. A cloud enveloped them, the air was electric, and the War Serpent made his presence felt.

Then the Shaman looked at me and spoke in perfect English.

"Kukulkan has been waiting for you. You are here for a reason. You are descended from Yax Pasah, the sixteenth King of Copan. All sixteen Mayan Kings are direct decedents of Yax Mo. Yax Pasah had the gift of tattoo. He was chosen by Kukulkan to carry the Mark of the Feathered Serpent. The spirit of Yax Pasah lives in you, and your spirit will be one with Kukulkan. Like your ancient father, you have the gift. You are to be trained. You too will carry the Mark of the Feathered Serpent and Kukulkan will guide your hands. Your training will begin in the temple in three days."

Luke listened to the Shamans words, but was emotionless. Then his eyes closed, his head fell back, and his face looked towards the sky. His lips began moving and he started praying, although no sound came out. Then he looked the Shaman in the eyes and began to speak Mayan, but in an ancient dialect that even Rosa didn't understand. The Shaman and Luke spoke in Mayan for some time, than they both went back into a trance that lasted several minutes. Finally, the presence faded, the heaviness lifted, and the room seemed to return to normal. The Shaman and Luke continued to talk for some time. Finally, they embraced and Luke was given his training schedule.

The Shaman sat and spoke with Rosa's family for a few minutes before he left, and then Rosa led everyone to their bedrooms to sleep off the Yage tea.

"Rosa was partially right," Luke thought to himself. *"We did get some answers, but we still didn't have the ink."*

Chapter 6

Early the next morning, Luke was awakened by the sound of laughter. As he opened his eyes, he felt the cool mountain breeze blowing through the window; and a warm glow from the morning sun that was rapidly filling the room.

He stumbled out of bed and found a basin of water on a table in the corner. He splashed the cold water on his face and dried it with a towel. As he was rubbing the sleep from his eyes, he felt somehow invigorated. He could vividly remember everything that happened the previous night, and had an unusually strong sense of well-being. Rosa was right. The Yagi tea had not hurt him.

He made my way to the kitchen where Jack and Max were having breakfast with Rosa and her family. They were serving eggs, plantains, tortillas, and coffee and everyone was laughing and having a great time. As usual, Max was telling jokes and had the whole group in stitches. There was also a lot of eye contact and even some flirting going on between Max and Rosa. The chemistry was strong and everyone could see it.

"Luke, what happened last night?"

"I don't know, Jack. One minute I'm on a 60's acid trip, and the next I'm talking to a god."

"What did god have to say?" Max said sarcastically. "I think we found out Luke is related to some ancient Mayan King."

"Isn't that nuts?" Jack laughed. "I mean, if I was related to some Mayan King, you'd think I would have known about it."

"Yeah," Luke said. "But I felt the hand of Kukulkan. I saw things I could have never have imagined. My eyes were opened. And I know this is going to sound nuts, but Kukulkan spoke to me through my mind. I never heard a voice, but my spirit touched his and I understood."

"What did you understand?" Max smirked.

"I understood what he wants me to do, Max. For some reason, I am here to do tattoos."

"Which tattoos?"

"I don't know, but that's what he said."

"What did the Shaman mean when he said they were going to train you?" Jack said.

"I don't know. But my training will start in three days. The Shaman also told me a Prince would help me."

"Did he tell you where you were going to find a Prince?" Max snarked.

"No Max. He said that the Prince will find me."

"Well, we'll see." Jack said. "In the meantime, Rosa, will you please tell your mother how much we enjoyed this breakfast." And even though her mother didn't speak a word of English, she was smiling and blushing as Jack poured on the charm and accolades.

After breakfast, they gathered their things to leave. The guards had spent the night alternately standing watch downstairs, and as they made their way out of town and back onto the highway, Luke was wondering how he was going to explain last night to Stacy.

About thirty-minutes out, as they were passing through a remote stretch of Highway 11, a large pickup was passing when it suddenly veered into them and forced them off the road. They hit a tree and the airbags deployed. When Luke opened his eyes, the cabin was filled with smoke from the airbags and tilting badly to one side. Before anyone had a chance to recover, the driver's door opened, and a man standing at the door began firing an automatic rifle into the front seat and killed both of the guards.

Suddenly, Luke's door flew open. The man with the gun started yelling in Spanish and motioning for everyone to get out of the vehicle. Five armed men surrounded them. They pulled all of them out of the truck and lined them up on their knees with their hands folded behind their heads.

Luke had never had a gun pointed at him before, and as he considered the possibility that he might not live to see the birth of his twins, a cold chill ran through his body and his eyes began to well up. He was scared to death.

The kidnappers bound everyone's hands tightly with rope and forced them into a van that had arrived on the scene while they were being tied up and blindfolded. They drove for about ten-minutes, and then pulled off the highway onto a dirt road that cut through the jungle. They made several turns, all the while dodging potholes and low-hanging branches. Eventually they came to a large clearing, which was obviously a camp. There was a couple of crude buildings surrounded by four large tents, and ten or more men milling about and watching the hostages with great interest.

As the van came to a stop, they were led into one of the tents. Their hands were still tied, and they were made to sit on the ground. Two men stayed in the tent with rifles to guard them. Up to now everyone had been too afraid to speak when Jack broke the silence with a whisper.

"You guys doing ok?"

"What are we going to do?" Max said.

"I'm pretty sure these guys want money and I'm going to give it to them," he answered.

One of the guards overheard them whispering and walked over. He pointed his rifle at Max's head and yelled at him in Spanish to be quiet. Then he kicked him just to make the point.

They sat on the ground in silence for an hour or so, when two more men came into the tent. They set up a table and four chairs. Then they pulled Rosa up off the ground and began to untie her. One of them looked at Rosa and said "El Bano," and she was led outside. When she returned, they sat her at the table and repeated the same process until everyone had been allowed to go to the bathroom and they were all seated at the table for dinner.

The two men who had set up the table began serving food. It was white rice and black beans, with slivers of pork and onions mixed in. They also had bread, butter and coffee. The group ate in silence, partially out of hunger and partially out of fear. They were allowed to talk at this point, but were afraid to be overheard by the guards. Gradually they loosened up and Max spoke first.

"Rosa, are you ok?"

"Yes. But I am scared to death. What are we going to do Max?" she asked with her voice cracking and tears starting to form in her eyes.

"We'll be ok. I don't think these guys want to hurt us or we'd be dead already. What they want is money, and lots of it. I suspect that somehow they found out Jack was coming to San Pedro Sula and have been following him, waiting for the right opportunity to take him. They know he's loaded and his family will pay a healthy ransom to get him back. But don't worry, we're going to give them whatever they want. It's only money."

Just then an older man who looked like he was in charge entered the tent. His continence was stoic, and he looked directly at Jack.

"Do you know why you're here Mr. Jennings?"

"I assume that you want money."

"You assume correctly. My employer has been following you since you landed in San Pedro Sula. You will bring a nice ransom."

"How much do you want?"

"You must remember, Mr. Jennings, I have no wish to

harm you. However, it has been my experience that when ransom terms are being negotiated, a finger or two from you will usually move the negotiations along quicker. But why go there. Your family will gladly pay to get you back in one piece."

"How much do you want?" Jack repeated the question.

"Five million US dollars and you can go home with all your fingers."

Jack closed his eyes and dropped his head. "Ok. But it'll take a day or two to make it happen. What about my friends?"

"Rosa is Mayan and is well known by my employer. She may go. One of my men will take her back to her father's house in the morning."

Rosa blurted out "Who's your employer? I want to know who's behind this."

"He is El Diablo, someone I believe you know."

"El Diablo! I should have known. This kidnapping has his stench all over it."

"What about Luke and Max?" Jack asked.

"That will be up to you, Mr. Jennings." The older man answered. "Tomorrow morning you will go back to San Pedro Sula with two of my men. You will contact your bank and arrange to have the money wired into my account. If you make any attempt to escape or call for help, we will kill your friends. They are worth nothing to me. What are they worth to you?"

"No, no. There won't be any need for that. I'll pay."

"That's very good, Mr. Jennings. I believe that we're starting to understand one another. Our business transaction may be beneficial to both of us. El Diablo gets the money, and you and your friends get to live."

We all just stared at the man, but nobody spoke. We were all in shock.

"I will let you get some rest now. We will speak again in the morning." And with that, the older man left the tent.

Two men came into the tent with cots. They assembled four cots with blankets and pillows, and motioned for everyone to go to bed. They had changed guards from earlier in the day, but continued to keep two armed guards in the tent with us at all times.

Max and Rosa had picked cots next to each other; and after the lights were dimed, Rosa reached over and took Max's hand. He squeezed her hand, and turned his head towards her. She did the same, and they laid on their cots in the semi-darkness staring into each other's eyes. She felt scared and vulnerable, and Max's calm demeanor was comforting. Later, Max would say he fell in love with Rosa that night.

Early the next morning Luke were awakened by roosters crowing. He and the others were allowed to go to the bathroom, and to wash with water in a bucket. Then they were seated back at the table and were served a breakfast of eggs, bread, mango, and coffee.

As they were finishing breakfast the older man entered the tent.

"Good morning Mr. Jennings. Did you sleep well?"

"Delightful accommodations," Jack answered.

"Yes, well, we have a big day planned for today. We have found some clothes that I believe will fit you. Once you get cleaned up, you and two of my men will go back to San Pedro Sula to take care of the money transfer. And do not forget. Any trouble from you and your friends will die."

Jack shaved and put on the clean clothes that had been provided. He was escorted to a truck by two armed guards, and they left for San Pedro Sula.

At the camp, all they could do was wait and hope for the best. They were allowed to walk around, and to sit on the cots or at the table, but had no communication with anyone or anything outside the tent.

Max stared at Rosa with a surprised look on his face and asked her "What did the older man mean when he said that you were well known to our kidnapper?"

"It's Miguel. Miguel Ortiz. And yes, we are very well acquainted. We knew each other in College at the Universidad de Honduras, but I became afraid of him."

"Why were you afraid of him?"

"It's his temper. When we first met he was very charming. We went to dinner a couple of times. I didn't want to be anything more than friends, and he seemed to be okay with that. But then he had an auto accident. It was bad. He was in the hospital for several weeks. He hit his head, and he was never the same. After the accident, he started losing his temper a lot, and over nothing. He would threaten people, and say the cruelest things. He decided I was his girlfriend. He stalked me day and night. He would even vandalize my property. I had the police investigate him, but they never found any evidence."

"How did you get away from him?" Max said.

"I was accepted into the Archeology program at the University of Miami, as a graduate student. After I came to the United States, we lost track of each other, and that was fine with me. Towards the end, I heard he had dropped out of school and started hanging out with a group of street tuffs. I heard that they were calling him El Diablo."

"Well, he obviously doesn't want to hurt you because you are being released." Max said.

"I'll believe it when I see it." Rosa said. "I guess all we can do now is wait."

Three hours later, Jack and his kidnappers arrived at the city. They drove down Boulevard Morazán to Citibank/Banco de Honduras. They parked and got out of the truck. As they prepared to go into the bank, one of the guards spoke into Jack's ear "Remember my friend, if you try to escape or call for help, I will go back to the camp and kill your friends."

"I'm not going to do anything. I just want to get you the money and get the hell out of here." Jack said.

They stepped away from the truck, and were walking towards the building when a volley of gunfire went off and killed both of the guards. The other people in the parking lot screamed and ran for their lives, but unfortunately, this is a regular occurrence in San Pedro Sula.

Almost immediately, a dark sedan with blacked out windows pulled up. The door opened, and Jack was ushered in and whisked away. There were three other men in the vehicle and he could hear the tires screech and feel the car lurch as it rapidly fled the scene before the police had a chance to arrive.

The driver looked back at Jack through the rear view mirror.

"Are you alright Mr. Jennings?"

"Yes, I think so. Who are you?"

"We work for Juan Rodriguez. We were sent here to rescue you."

"Yes, you are under the protection of the Prince" said the man sitting next to Jack.

"What do mean *the Prince*?"

"Senor Rodriguez. That's what they call him, the Prince of the city."

"And where are you taking me?"

"Senor Rodriguez wants to meet you. He is planning a raid on El Diablo's camp to rescue your friends."

"Thank God," Jack said. And as the sedan drove through the city, he laid his head back into the seat, closed his eyes, and breathed a sigh of relief.

Chapter 7

It only took about ten-minutes to reach their destination. The sedan pulled into a parking garage and then drove to a private entrance. The driver opened the gate with his access card. Once in, he found a parking space near the elevators. There were two security guards there to screen everyone entering the Prince's personal office suites.

After being cleared to enter, they boarded the elevator and pressed the button for the top floor. The man with the access card inserted it into the elevator, and it allowed them to enter the top three floors where the Prince's office suites and Penthouse are located.

The elevator took Jack from the parking garage to the top floor of the building. They walked down a hallway filled with Mayan artwork that led to a set of giant golden doors. As the doors were opened, Jack entered the room.

Behind an ornate desk sat a man who appeared to be in his early to mid-thirties. He was impeccably dressed, and he stood to greet Jack when he entered the room. His office was finished in a style that could best be described as Mayan Contemporary. But the most striking thing about his office was the glass wall. From his perch on the twentieth floor, Jack could see the entire city. The glass covered the entire back wall of the Prince's office and the view of San Pedro Sula was spectacular.

He reached out to shake Jack's hand.

"Are you hurt?"

Jack was surprised by how fluent his English was.

"I am Juan Rodriguez," he said. "Please sit down," as he directed Jack to the sofa. "May I fix you something to drink?"

"Sure," responded Jack.

"What happened to you was unfortunate. Our country can be a dangerous place. But we need to get back to El Diablo's camp where your friends are being held. When the two men who brought you here don't show back up with you, they might kill one or both of your friends."

"How will you find them?"

"We already know where they are. I have a man on the inside who feeds me information. Greed can be a powerful motivator" the Prince said.

"Yes it can, and so can fear. And right now my friends are very fearful that they may not get out of there alive. How're you going to get them out?"

"We'll land a couple of helicopters in the middle of the

camp and do a military style extraction" the Prince said. "Many of my men have military training, and have extensive experience in dealing with this kind of thing."

"This feels like a nightmare you can't wake up from." Jack said.

"What brought you here?"

"It's the tattoos. I've become fascinated with the tattoos. We came down here looking for the tattoo ink I've seen in pictures" Jack said. "The colors are the most beautiful I've ever seen."

"Yes," the Prince said, at which he rolled up his shirt sleeve to reveal a tattoo of an arrow in flight, tattooed on the inside of his forearm. "It is The Mark of Ah Tabai, the god of the hunt. It channels the hunter's spirit with Ah Tabai, and guides our arrows swift and straight. It has a sacred meaning to our people."

"Can I get a closer look?" Jack asked, and then wondered out loud "where did they get the ink?"

"The Shaman makes it from the clay and flowers that you can only find in Copan," the Prince said.

"How can I get some of the ink?" asked Jack.

"The tattoos can only be done by a Shaman, or a Master of Tattoo, and Kukulkan will guide the Shaman so he will know which tattoos have his blessing."

"What's it going to take for me to be considered?" Jack said.

"Kukulkan grants blessings and protections as he sees fit. A Shaman or Master of Tattoo will only tattoo those whom Kukulkan has chosen. But let's turn our attention to your friends."

"Did Max hire you to preform security?" Jack asked.

"Yes, and I am disappointed that El Diablo's men were able to kidnap you. We protect many important visitors to San Pedro Sula, and rarely do we have a problem. My company provides corporate services, guarding important shipments of goods and data. We also provide protection for executives. However, the further you go up into the mountains, the harder it is to protect you."

"Our raiding party will leave here in thirty-minutes." the Prince said. "It is a twenty-minute flight by helicopter to reach the camp. I expect heavy resistance, so I am taking ten men and two helicopters with me. Hopefully we can take out El Diablo's men and have your friends on a flight back to Copan in time for supper."

"I'm going with you" Jack said.

"I don't think so. This raid will be dangerous and people may die on both sides. We might have to do some ugly things to rescue your friends. I can't allow it."

"If I paid for your security services, then you work for me. My friends are being held at gunpoint in that camp and I'm going. Get me a gun."

The Prince stopped momentarily. There was a puzzled look on his face because he was not used to being questioned or challenged, and it caught him off guard. He seemed almost amused and smiled. "Ok, I don't have time to argue with you. If we don't do something right now, at least one and maybe both of your friends will be dead before the day is over; I will not abandon them to El Diablo. But you go at your own risk and you will ride with me. This is not negotiable." Then he turned around and said to one of his men "get him a gun, and whatever else he's going to need. We meet on the roof in fifteen-minutes." Then he looked to one of his other men and said, "Stay with him and make sure he gets there."

Jack had been outfitted and was being led to the rooftop when he began to hear a low rumble. The closer he got, the louder it got. When he reached the stairs that lead to the rooftop, the whole stairway was vibrating and the sound became overwhelming. When he got to the roof, he realized that the sound was coming from two very large helicopters that were standing by for the Prince.

As his assault team reached the top of the stairs, they hurried across the roof and got into the helicopters. Jack stayed with the Prince and the two of them boarded the lead chopper.

As their helicopter began to lift off the roof, the pilot turned around and spoke to them with a pronounced American accent.

"Good morning Boss."

"Good morning Mike. Let's go get some bad guys."

"Aye, Captain." Mike said. And with that he raised the big bird off the ground, turned the nose up, and took her out.

As they climbed over the city, everyone sat in silence. They all knew what they had to do. They flew over the mountains and followed the river until they had nearly reached their objective. Then Mike radioed back to the other chopper *"Touchdown in four minutes."* He cut a hard left and began to descend on the jungle.

After a few minutes they reached the camp, and both

choppers hovered momentarily. Jack had been able to a draw a picture of the camp, so the Prince had a pretty good idea of which tent the captives were in. When the helicopters touched down, three of the Prince's men leaped out of the helicopter and lay prone on the ground. They began to fire on El Diablo's men, which gave Jack and the Prince the opportunity to make a dash for the tent where the others were being held.

Back inside the tent, Max nudged Luke on the shoulder and said "Luke, look."

The two men who had been guarding Max, Rosa and I turned their backs on us to look out the tent at the helicopters. When they did, that gave Max the opportunity he'd been waiting for. He leaped upon the two guards and unloaded a flurry of kicks and punches, and within about fifteen-seconds, he had moped up the floor with both of them.

I stared in amazement at the way Max handled those guys.

Max just shrugged it off and gave me a smile.

I picked up the rifle that one of the guards had dropped. I cocked it and pulled a bullet into the chamber. Max did the same and grabbed Rosa. They stood by the tent door to follow the situation outside. The Prince's men were pouring out of the choppers and into the camp.

The Prince and Jack ran into the tent where Max, Rosa

and Luke were being held.

"Oh, thank God you are here," Rosa said with tears in her eyes.

"Get down, get down. Move back," The Prince kept saying.

The fighting outside the tent raged on. The Prince stayed in the front to guard his charges, but kept watch out the door at each step of the way. I squatted in the back of the tent, grasping the rifle I had taken from the unconscious guard.

I held the rifle tightly. My hands were wet with sweat, my heart pounded, and my breathing was coming in short quick bursts. Could I use the rifle if I had to? Could I take a life, even in self-defense? I wasn't sure.

Suddenly, Luke heard the sound of canvas being cut, and when he turned around he could see that one of El Diablo's men was cutting his way through the wall of the tent with a knife. Without hesitating, Luke fired. He shot the man in the chest, right through the tent at close range, and his body was thrown back three-feet or more before he hit the ground.

Everyone turned around and looked, then turned back around to watch the front of the tent without saying a word.

The Prince walked to the door and said "Don't go anywhere." And with that he bolted out of the tent and into the battle.

Jack, Max and Luke were all armed and guarded the door while watching the corners of the tent for any more *cutters*. Still, the battle raged on and bursts of gunfire filled the air. Luke saw some of the Princes men pin down two kidnappers. There was a back and forth gun fight until one of the kidnappers was wounded and the other dead.

Finally, the shooting began to subside. From Luke's vantage point inside the tent, he could see the Prince standing in the field, directing the evacuation of the wounded. One of his men was killed, and another three wounded. In addition, four of El Diablo's men were killed, and another five wounded. So the Prince had the wounded all loaded into one chopper and dispatched them to the hospital in San Pedro Sula.

The older man who seemed to be in charge was one of El Diablo's men who survived the raid. They would be loaded into vans with their hands tied, and driven back into the city by the Prince's assault team. There they were turned over to the police, as well as the four dead bodies of El Diablo's men.

Jack, Max, Rosa and Luke were all loaded into the second chopper. As we lifted up, Luke's heart was still beating out of his chest and his breathing was quick. Mike took the chopper airborne, where it banked and climbed over the jungle until at last they arrived in Copan.

Back at the Hacienda San Lucas, Jack and Luke were reunited with our terrified wives.

Rosa was visibly shaken and clung to Max. He walked her back to her trailer in the archeologist village, then stood outside and held her. She looked at Max with tears in her eyes, and then she kissed him. Max looked deep into her eyes and kissed her back. Then he told her goodnight, kissed her again, and walked back to the hotel.

All the way back, he kept asking himself "Did that really happen?"

Later that evening, as Luke lay in bed with Stacy, he tried to make sense of the last two days. He had met a Shaman, took a hallucinogenic drug, and spoke to a god. He was kidnapped, and then killed a man in a gunfight. He was almost killed. Then he was rescued, flown away in a helicopter, and tomorrow he would start his Tattoo training with the Shaman.

He was getting more than he bargained for.

Chapter 8

The next morning, Luke was nervous. He barely slept the night before. He didn't know what to expect, and he had mixed feelings. On the one hand, he was curious about what his training would entail. On the other hand, he feared what might happen.

Once Stacy and Mary had heard of the abduction, they were both ready to pack it up and go home. But there was no way Luke or Jack were going to leave Honduras without some of that ink.

Max had his own reasons to stay. Things were really starting to heat up with Rosa. The flirting escalated, and although they had only known each other for a few days, everyone could see the attraction.

While Luke was receiving his training, Max spent the day helping Rosa recover from their ordeal. He also needed to handle Jack's business affairs, which didn't stop just because he came to Honduras.

Jack and Mary spent the day at the hotel resting.

Luke's instructions were to be at the Temple at seven and to fast overnight. He made his way to the Temple at the appointed time and went around back to a restricted entrance where Dario, the Shaman's apprentice, was waiting to escort him in.

He reached out, touching the limestone blocks of the passage walls as they entered. The stones were cold and damp. It was a chill that set the tone for the seriousness of what was to come. Shivers of both excitement and apprehension ran down his spine.

The archeology teams had burrowed out passageways through the stone walls of the temple to allow access to key areas without destroying important structures and artifacts. Dario and Luke found their way through the tunnel by torchlight, and came to a hidden stairway that led them into a large ceremonial chamber that was also lit by torchlight.

There was the tranquil sound of water flowing through the chamber from a crystal pure underground spring, and the walls were covered with murals depicting everything from bloody battle scenes, to everyday life in a Mayan village. And although archeologists had long considered the Mayans to be peace loving star gazers, the murals on this wall told another story. There were pictures of Mayan warriors torturing, killing, and dismembering their enemies. Others depicted human sacrifice. One picture showed a Mayan Shaman cutting out a man's heart. But the really amazing thing was the paint. The colors looked incredible, even though the murals were painted over a thousand years ago.

Luke entered the chamber with Dario and was instructed to sit on a mat that had been provided for him. Dario appeared to be in his early twenties, and accompanied the Shaman almost everywhere. As the Shaman's apprentice, he was being prepared for the day that the Mayan Council of Elders decided he was ready to assume the duties of a Shaman.

On that particular day he was preparing the ink.

The fire pit sat in the corner of the chamber. It was made of stone and inset into the floor. The top protruded up from the floor about three-feet, and there was a two-inch lip around the edge to set the stone bowl on. Next to the fire pit were bowls which had been hollowed out of stone. The Shaman's apprentice had two stone rods, chiseled from solid rock, that were used to place and remove the stone bowls from atop the fire pit.

Dario didn't speak a word of English, and yet he and Luke were able to communicate without saying a word. Dario's spirit spoke to Luke's spirit, and he understood everything that Dario said.

Luke was invited me to step closer and observe the making of the ink. The Shaman's apprentice was careful to explain what he was doing at each step, and to make sure that Luke understood each step before he moved on.

Dario reached into a wooden bucket, grabbed a handful of clay, and placed it in the stone bowl. He picked up a handful of red flowers which he also placed in the bowl. He blended the ingredients, carefully lifting the stone bowl with the stone rods and gently placing it atop the fire pit. Then he set the stone rods aside.

Luke watched the clay begin to melt. It turned white, then into a paste. At the same time, the flowers burned and dissolved almost immediately. But the ash was red instead of black, and when it burned the red pigment spread through the clay and turned it red. The whole process took seconds, and when it was over, we had a bowl of red paste.

Dario used the stone rods to pick the bowl up and set it off to the side. The stone bowl was white hot, and would take almost an hour to cool enough that it could be handled.

Dario repeated the process several times, using the same clay, but different colored flowers to make different colored inks. He would then set the bowls aside until he had all the colors necessary for the tattoo they were doing that day. Then they rested and meditated until the bowls cooled.

Once the bowls were cool enough to touch, Dario picked up a pitcher and walked over to the stream. He dipped the pitcher in the water, and carried it back to the stone bowls. He slowly poured the water into the bowl, blending the water and the red paste until it became ink.

He repeated the process several more times, making several bowls of different color inks. Then he invited Luke to help.

"This is unbelievable" Luke thought to himself. *"I came here to find the ink, and here I am making ink with the Shaman's apprentice."*

After he finished helping Dario, they both continued to rest and meditate until the Shaman arrived. As he entered the chamber, Dario stood and bowed, as did Luke. There were cushions on the floor for the Shaman, Dario and Luke, and one for the man being tattooed, who would arrive later. The Shaman greeted them and they all sat down.

The Shaman said nothing, but closed his eyes and

lifted his face towards the heavens. He began to pray, and as he did, heaviness descended on the chamber. The air became thick and electric, yet Luke's senses were crystal clear. Dario and Luke were both drawn into a trance as a cloud enveloped the room. They began to pray as well, although Luke didn't understand what he was saying. Then gradually he found himself levitating as his whole body was lifted off the ground.

An invisible presence filled the room, slowly at first, then accelerating rapidly. As it did, the Shaman began chanting a prayer in Mayan, but this time Luke understood every word; and then it happened – Luke's mind was opened again, and he heard the voice of Kukulkan speaking to his heart.

"Son of Yax Pasah. Like your ancient grandfather, you have the spirit of a warrior and a healer. You have been anointed to carry the Mark of the Feathered Serpent. I will lead you to those I have chosen. I will guide your hand and open your mind. I will strengthen you for battle, and you will become a tool in my hands."

With that, the Shaman lifted his face to the heavens and continued praying for several more minutes, then closed his eyes and sat in silence. Shortly, the presence that had filled the room left. The heaviness lifted, and all things returned to normal.

The Shaman looked at Luke and said, "It is time for your training to begin."

He opened a leather bag and laid it on the chamber floor. Inside the bag were numerous tools that were the tattoo instruments. The Shaman told Luke what each tool was for, and how to use it. And although he spoke very little English, the Shaman was still able to communicate directly with Luke's spirit. He never heard a voice, yet he understood every word the Holy Man said.

As the Shaman was finishing his explanation, a man appeared at the chamber entrance. He was being led by what appeared to be another one of the Shaman's assistants.

They bowed to the Shaman, entered the room and sat down. There were a few words spoken in Mayan between the Shaman and the man, and then the tattooing started.

Dario rubbed oil on the spot where the tattoo would go. The man was getting the Mark of Jerkewitz, mountain god of the K'iche', used to help mountain guides find their way through the jungle.

The Shaman picked up the first tool. It was a long, sharp needle made from bone. One end was flat from tapping it with a mallet. He dipped the sharp end of the needle into the black ink and positioned it on the man's forearm where the tattoo was to go. He picked up the mallet and began tapping the needle into the man's flesh. As the ink found its way under the man's skin you could see a metamorphosis occur. The ink seemed to glow right through the man's flesh. It was almost as if the ink were alive. And as the Shaman continued his work, the tattoo's colors became even brighter, much like the one's Luke had seen in the pictures Stacy's Uncle had sent.

The continuous tap, tap, tap of the mallet on the needle was the only sound in the chamber and was amplified by the stone walls. Periodically, the Shaman would stop tapping long enough to wipe away the excess ink and blood.

Luke had known about the ancient art of tattooing with these crude instruments, but this was the first time he had actually seen it done. He knew that it must be extremely painful, but the man never showed any sign of it. He sat quietly the whole time without so much as a frown.

When the tattoo's outline was complete, everyone stood to stretch their legs. Dario served water, and gave the man who was being tattooed a towel so he could wipe away the perspiration that was beginning to flow as a result of the pain he was experiencing. Apparently, you can play a porker face under extreme pain, but your body will give you away every time

After a short rest period, everyone sat back down and resumed the work. This time the Shaman picked up a different tool, and dipped it into the stone bowl that contained the blue ink. This tool was smaller, also made of bone. It had an extremely sharp flat tongue that extended out about an inch, and was used to lift the skin so the ink could be evenly distributed. The Shaman had Luke help finish the Tattoo as he supervised the effort. And the whole time he was doing the tattoo, Kukulkan guided his hand.

After some time everyone stood up again to stretch their legs for a second time. And once again, the Shaman's assistants gave the man who was being tattooed water and a clean towel to wipe the sweat that was now pouring out of him from pain.

The Shaman picked up still another instrument. This one was like a very small razor blade that would deposit the colored ink under the skin. Once again, the Shaman dipped the instrument into the ink, and set it on the skin. He picked up the mallet and started tapping again. Luke thought to himself that the pain must surely be intense, but again, the man never showed any sign of it.

His wife had been allowed to enter the chamber to comfort him. She held his hand, and spoke comforting words into his ears. Once the Shaman had deposited three or four wads of ink under the skin, he lifted the skin with a tool, and pushed the ink around under the skin until he got even distribution. Once again, the man being tattooed never made a sound, but this time tears began to run down his face. But still, he never said a word.

The Shaman put the mallet into Luke's hand and tapped him on the arm lightly to demonstrate how hard he should hit the tool as he was tattooing the man. Then he motioned for Luke to take over. And although he had done hundreds of tattoos over the years, he had never done one like this.

When he dipped the tattoo tool into the blue ink, Luke noticed his hand was shaking. But as his hand drew near the tattoo, it stopped shaking as the spirit of Kukulkan guided him.

Soon Luke was tapping. He deposited the ink three times, then lifted the skin with the special tool and made sure that the ink was evenly distributed. He went on in this manner for about an hour, until the area he was working on was completely covered. Periodically, they would take a break to stretch their legs, and then they were right back at it.

Finally, with help from the Shaman, Luke finished the tattoo. The man who was tattooed needed help to leave, and his arm was swollen, but the tattoo was the most beautiful work Luke had ever done. It was the ink, and Kukulkan had guided his hand.

When he returned to the hotel, Stacy was waiting for him with a dozen questions. "What happened? How did you feel? Did you find the ink?"

She besieged him with questions, but he had no

answers. He had no words to adequately describe what happened. But as he did his best to recount the events of his first training day, he kept coming back to the fact that he had heard the voice of Kukulcan, and that the War Serpent had guided his hand.

Chapter 9

The Prince arranged for everyone to fly back to San Pedro Sula for dinner later that evening. He sent a van to pick them up and they drove to a clearing about five miles south of Copan. He had two helicopters waiting to take everyone back to the city. When they reached the clearing, everyone got out of the van and ran across the open field. They found their way into one of the two choppers and strapped themselves in.

The chopper lifted up off the ground slowly and took them out into the night sky. The only light in the cockpit was coming from the pilot's instruments and gauges.

After twenty-minutes in the air, Luke could see the lights of San Pedro Sula in the distance. As they flew over the city, it was like flying over a giant pinball machine. The digital billboards lit up the night sky along with neon lights reflecting off glass and chrome buildings. The helicopter set down on top of the same building where Jack had originally met the Prince, and they were ushered to the elevator and down the hall to his office.

The Prince stood up to greet them as they entered. He invited them to sit down and had one of his men take drink orders. Luke sat on the couch looking out over the city from the giant window that covered the entire back wall of the Prince's office. He couldn't help being intrigued by the raw beauty of the place. It belied the fact San Pedro Sula is so dangerous.

As they entered the room, Stacy introduced the Prince to her Uncle Robert.

"Uncle Robert, I'd like you to meet Juan Rodriguez."

Stacy's Uncle extended his hand towards the Prince, then turned towards Rosa and said "Oh yes, and I'd like you to meet Dr. Lazaro."

"We are well acquainted." said the Prince. "We have worked together several times at charity events for the Mayan Children's Relief Fund."

Rosa hugged the Prince and gave him a kiss on the cheek."

"It's nice to see you again, Juan"

"And you as well, Rosa. Or is it Dr. Lazaro now."

"She just completed her Doctoral program at the University of Miami and will be joining the faculty as an Associate Professor in the fall." said Uncle Robert.

"Until yesterday, it had been several years since I have seen you Rosa. I'm glad that you are doing well in Miami."

Then the Prince turned to Jack and said "This must be Mary."

"It's nice to meet you Juan. Tell me about the Mayan Children's Relief Fund."

"It's a project near and dear to my heart. We are heavily dependent on corporate sponsorships, but have been overwhelmed by the generosity of the Honduran people. One-hundred percent of all monies collected go straight to the children. I sit on the board, and every year we strive to expand our relief zone, but it will never be enough until every Mayan child has enough food to eat."

They made small talk as the Prince's staff served drinks and appetizers. After fifteen-minutes, a gentleman wearing a tuxedo appeared at the door of the Prince's office and announced dinner was ready to be served. Everyone stood and followed the Prince down the hall and into the most incredible dining room any of them had ever seen.

The room was dimly lit and spacious. The outside wall in the dining room was made entirely of glass, like the Prince's office, and offered a breathtaking view of the city. The room is centered on a large mahogany table which seats at least twenty guests with ease. The floor is wooden, and there is a large, elegant multi-colored silk rug under the table. There was a multitude of strategically placed candles, and a crystal chandelier that's a piece of art in its own right. The room was filled with Mayan art and relics, with spot lighting to provide the optimal light for each piece. There was a two-foot statue of Yax Kuk Mo, the first king of Copan, made of solid gold. There were numerous statues of animals, in various sizes, made entirely of gold or jade. There were also several jade statues of the feathered serpent, with gold inlay; and a display of ancient Mayan weapons and body armor.

Uncle Robert almost fell down when he saw the Prince's collection. "My God, man; these are museum pieces. Your collection is spectacular."

Uncle Robert had never seen a private collection like this that one, and in such good condition.

"I think it would be safe to say that there is not another collection like this in the world. The artwork and weapons on display in this dining room are better than many pieces found in museums."

Rosa was also taken aback. "I've not seen a collection like this anywhere."

"Thank you, my friends," the Prince replied. "The artwork tells the story of the Maya."

Uncle Robert was speechless. He walked over to a display that held a war club with extremely sharp spikes coming out.

"This battle club, for instance. Where in the world did you find this piece in such good condition?"

"It was a gift from General Garcia of the Honduran Army. He gave it to me in appreciation for my company's help with security during a coup attempt."

"I've never seen one in this condition," Uncle Robert said.

"Would you like to hold it?" the Prince asked. And without waiting for Stacy's uncle to reply, he walked over to the display where Uncle Robert was standing. He reached inside, picked up the weapon, and handed it to him.

Uncle Robert was stunned.

"How old is this?" Uncle Robert asked.

"I am told it comes from the burial tomb of 18 Rabbit, the powerful and much beloved thirteenth King of Copan. He reigned from six-ninety-five to seven-thirty-eight" the Prince answered, "so it was probably made in the early seven-hundreds. Oh yes, and be very careful with that battle club you're holding, it is very sharp."

Rosa was mesmerized by a Jade necklace.

"Professor Nolan, did you see this necklace?"

"It's a beautiful piece," said Mary who walked over to get a closer view.

"Yes," said Uncle Robert. "The Mayans valued jade even more than gold and silver. They considered it to be sacred and holy."

"It is the ultimate symbol of all that is good, including eternal love" said the Prince.

"Surely this necklace must have belonged to a queen" Rosa said.

"Well then, Professor Lazaro; it's obvious that we're going to have to get you one of these necklaces." Max said as he smiled and looked right at Rosa.

The staff began serving dinner, so everyone sat down and ate. As they did, the Prince told them about the Mayan people living here today.

"There are still over seven million of us still living in Central America."

"Yes, and their conditions are very poor" said Rosa. "Most of them live in small villages in the mountains, surrounded by dense jungles. The children cannot read because they have no schools. People die needlessly because they have no access to basic medical care. They don't have enough food or shelter, and little hope of improving their situation without help from the outside."

"It has been my mission to improve the lives of my people. My security company allows me the finances and the freedom to help these mountain villagers build schools and clinics. This is the most important work I do, and I will never stop as long as I have breath in my body."

"What can we do to help?" Mary offered.

"Where do you want to start?" the Prince answered with a smile. "You should come up to the mountains with me tomorrow. I have a team going up there with a food shipment and you could get a look for yourself."

"I'd love to. What time are you leaving?" said Mary.

"We're leaving here with two trucks and a Jeep around nine o'clock. Why don't I have a helicopter pick you up in Copan at 8:30 and fly you here so we can all leave together?" the Prince answered.

"That'll be great." Mary said.

"What about you Jack? Do you want to come?" the Prince continued.

"Yeah, I'd love to visit a couple of these remote villages, just to get a sense of the Mayan people; who they are, what we have in common. Sure, I'll go."

"What about you Luke?" the Prince asked.

"Tomorrow I'm being trained by the Shaman. I can't miss a single day" he said.

"I'm a little nervous for him," said Stacy. "Tomorrow he's to be tattooed and I understand this traditional way of tattooing is very painful."

"Not everyone can endure the process" Rosa said.

"Yes," Luke conceded. "But shouldn't the Tattoo Master understand the pain?"

"Yes," agreed the Prince.

"I agree too," said Stacy. "I'm sure he'll do well tomorrow. I've tattooed Luke several times, and he's always done great. Not even a frown."

"Would you like to come as well?" the Prince asked Stacy.

"Ok. Maybe there's something I can do to help."

"I'm sure we can come up with something," said the Prince with a smile.

"How about you Max? Do you want to go?"

"Rosa, are you going?" Max asked her.

"Sure Max, I'll go," she said.

"Ok then, count me in." he said.

"How about you Uncle Robert, would you like to go?" Stacy asked.

"Thank you, Stacy, but no. I have work to be done that can't wait. Besides, Dr. Lazaro is more than capable of providing you with all the archeological information you will need."

When dinner was over, they adjourned to a private

lounge, which was adjacent to the dining room. The Prince's bartenders kept the drinks flowing and they smoked fine cigars from his private humidor. The whole group laughed uncontrollably as Max, who was more than a little intoxicated, started telling jokes and doing impressions.

Luke had seen him do this a couple of times before, and while he always thought Max was funny, that night he was hilarious. They were all laughing so hard they could barely catch their breath.

Later that evening, on the flight back to Copan, Luke's mind began to wander back to his tattoo shop in Miami. He had been gone for less than a week, and yet it seemed like another lifetime ago.

The next morning, Luke met Dario at the back entrance of the temple. They made their way through the tunnel and down the stairway into the ceremonial chamber. The Shaman was waiting for them when he got there. The ink had been prepared by Dario, and the tattoo instruments were laid out on the floor.

Luke was instructed to sit down. The room was silent and no one dared to speak. Shortly, the Shaman, Dario, and Luke began to chant and pray in Mayan. They fell into a trance, only this time Luke was able to understand a few words.

Heaviness fell on the chamber and the air became electric. A cloud enveloped the room, and Luke felt his body being raised off the floor again. The presence of Kukulkan filled the place, and he spoke to Luke through the Shaman in an ancient Mayan dialect.

They continued to chant and pray Mayan prayers until gradually the presence of Kukulkan faded, the heaviness lifted and the room returned to normal.

The Shaman looked at Luke and spoke in Mayan, and in his spirit, Luke understood every word.

"Today you will learn about the Butterfly of Life. Kukulkan will speak to you and you will know who to heal. The power to heal carries a heavy responsibility. Only the gods know when it is a man's time to die. The Master of Tattoo must be sure he hears their voices."

The Shaman continued to speak as two men arrived at the cavern's entrance carrying another man who was obviously very ill. They waited for permission to enter. Dario nodded, so they carried in the man who was to be tattooed and laid him on the mat.

The Shaman picked up his tattoo needle and mallet, dipped the needle in black ink, and began tapping the tattoo's outline. Luke assisted, and the Shaman guided him at each step of the way.

Luke tapped in a good portion of the tattoo, and as he did, the man began to get noticeably better. The colors came alive as they touched his skin, and as each piece of the butterfly was completed, the man continued to show improvement. By the end, he was sitting up and appeared to be completely healed.

When the tattoo was complete, he stood up and walked around the room. Both he and his friends were overcome with joy and continued to thank the Shaman over and over. Finally, after they left, the Shaman turned his attention to Luke.

"Today you are to receive the Mark of the McCaw, the

sign of the Master of Tattoo. You will continue your training for another five days. During that time the Mark of the McCaw will meld with your skin and link your spirit to Kukulkan. Only then can the will of Kukulkan flow through your hands. Until then, you are to do no tattoos without the Shaman unless instructed to do so."

The Shaman picked up the tattoo needle, dipped it in the ink, and began outlining the Mark of the McCaw on Luke's hand. And although a tattoo on the hand with the needle and mallet is excruciating, he never made a sound. Instead, he thought of Stacy and our unborn babies, and how excited she had been that morning to visit the mountain villages and to see the children.

When it was over, the Shaman helped Luke pack some of the ink that had been prepared for him. He packed it, along with needles and mallets, into a leather satchel that he was instructed to carry with him everywhere he went.

Earlier that same day, the Prince had sent a van to pick everyone up at the hotel at eight-thirty. They had driven to the clearing, boarded the chopper, and within thirty-minutes they were standing in the Prince's office.

"Good morning, my friends," the Prince said. "How is everyone doing?"

"Great," said Jack, "and we're looking forward to visiting the villages."

"Good." said the Prince. "Both of these trucks are

loaded with food and supplies, so let's get started."

Ten-minutes into the drive, the Prince turned to Jack and asked if he had seen the morning news yet.

"No, why do you ask?" Jack said.

"In San Pedro Sula this morning, a man got into an argument with a waitress over a plate of eggs and he started yelling like a crazy man. Apparently, he leaped out of the booth and grabbed the waitress by the neck. He started slamming her face into the table until she was unrecognizable. Eye witnesses say he pulled out a gun and began shooting the other customers. They said he shot and killed five people before he turned the gun on himself."

"What do you make of it?" I wondered.

"It has to be the Curse," said the Prince. "That's the only thing that will make a man that evil. Reporters on the scene are saying he had a tattoo of a snake with feathers on the inside of his forearm; and I just found out this morning El Diablo has a rogue Shaman who knows how to make the ink and is trying to tattoo the Mark of the Feathered Serpent on his men. I heard that he's planning to tattoo as many of his men as possible and create an army of supermen." the Prince said.

"Don't they realize that they're going to bring on the Curse? Nobody can tattoo the Mark of the Feathered Serpent without the blessing of Kukulcan" Rosa said. "But I can tell you what's going to happen," she added. "His rogue Shaman is going to create monsters while he is trying to figure out how to make the ink outside of the temple. I don't think it can done, and we'll end up with God only knows how many homicidal maniacs walking the streets."

"How can we stop him?" Jack said.

"That's the problem. We don't how many of these maniacs there are, or where they are. I think I'll have a tough time defending the population. And, of course, we need to find that Shaman. I'm hoping citizens will report suspicious activity and we can stop him from killing any more innocent people." said the Prince.

Mary and Stacy talked all the way there, while staring out the windows and commenting on the unbelievably beautiful scenery. They were ignoring the conversation about homicidal maniacs and thinking about seeing the village children.

They took CA 4 and headed north. At San Mateo, they picked up HRT 80 and headed deeper up into the mountains. They were surrounded by dense jungle and the road became more and more difficult to navigate. They traveled for over an hour before they came to a fork in the road. They took the left fork, and after twenty-minutes of navigating the jungle roads, they came to the village of San Luis.

San Luis is a small village with roughly seventy-five men, women, and children. As the Prince's team pulled their vehicles into the center of the village, the children came running out to greet them. The Prince had been going there for several years and made a difference you could see and feel. The children were clean and well dressed. They were well fed and looked healthy and happy. You could see that the people of the village loved the Prince, and that the feeling was mutual.

The village was charming, and the people were gentle and welcoming to strangers. Up there, they are out of the gang violence and constant fear that comes from living in San Pedro Sula.

Last year, the Prince brought in a construction team with heavy equipment, and within a few weeks had built ten family residences, a dorm for temporary housing, a storehouse, and a one-room schoolhouse which also doubled as a clinic.

As they were climbing out of their vehicles, the village Chief came out to greet them. He hugged the Prince and was anxious to show him some recent improvements to the village. In the meantime, some of the village men began unloading the truck and carrying the food and supplies into the storehouse.

Several of the village children came up to Stacy and began speaking all at once in Mayan. They were smiling and laughing, and made her smile as well to see the pure innocence of these beautiful children.

Mary was especially touched as she got on one knee and hugged the children who were all excited to see a pretty lady from a faraway land. She and Stacy had visited the hotel gift shop that morning and bought up all the candy they had to give away to the children.

The Prince walked over to Mary and said, "This is why I do what I do." And over the next hour or so they visited as many of the families as they could, and every one hugged the Prince and thanked him over and over for what he had done for their village.

After the supplies were unloaded, they had lunch with the Chief and a few of the village elders. They discussed the Prince's plan to bring in a medical missionary team to visit the village. He had a commitment they were coming in the spring; he just didn't have a firm date yet. After lunch the village children sang a song in Mayan that they had prepared for the Prince; and after they had a chance to say goodbye to everybody, the team climbed back into their vehicles and headed back out towards CA 4.

"I'm really glad you had a chance to visit the village" said the Prince. "They've come a long way, but we still have a lot of work to do. I'm going to do everything I can to help them."

"Jack and I would love to do something to help" Mary said.

"There are dozens of other villages, just like this one, who lack the basic essentials of life: food, housing, medical care and education. Now we are on our way to visit another village, La Paz that we have just recently started working with" said the Prince. "These poor people have nothing, but we're going to fix that."

After an hour and a half, they arrived in La Paz. They pulled their vehicles into the middle of the village, but unlike San Luis, the children were nowhere to be found, and people looked at them with suspicion.

As they were getting out of the trucks, the village Chief came to greet them. He had spoken to the Prince previously about delivering some food to the village. Some of the village men started unloading the truck, and carrying the food and supplies into a large hut they used as a storehouse. He and the Chief went around the village, speaking with the families. Later they sat down and talked about plans to improve the village.

As we pulled away, many of the village children came out to see us off. All the way home, Mary and Stacy just gushed.

"Jack and I want to help." Mary said

"That is very generous Mrs. Jennings. With your NFL connections you could be a very effective fundraiser."

"I'll do what I can." Mary said. "Jack and I don't mind getting our hands dirty either."

Stacy wanted to help as well, and all the way home, spirits were high as everyone thought of ways to bring comfort to the children of Honduras.

Chapter 11

Jack and Mary had been married for over twelve years, and since the beginning they've always had a weekly "date night" whenever possible. Usually, it's on a Monday night, because that's often the only day Jack has off during football season. And of course, there were times they couldn't because of one reason of another. But they always made their relationship a priority.

Against the advice of the Prince, Max made reservations for Jack and Mary at El Restaurante Donnie's. It was considered by many to be the finest steak house in San Pedro Sula, and a favorite of the city's upper class. There's almost always a two week wait for reservations, but the Prince managed to get them a table, and they went despite the security concerns.

Even though he was retired from the day to day operation of the restaurant, Donnie could still be found there several nights a week, greeting old friends and making new ones. He'd roll up his sleeves in the kitchen to train promising chiefs, and pass his secret recipes down to the next generation. He was like a father to many of his employees and a local celebrity there in San Pedro Sula.

The restaurant manager had seated Jack and Mary at a corner table, and the security guards at the table next to them. They were as inconspicuous as possible, but kept a constant eye on the room.

Donnie was there that night, so after they were seated and had a chance to order drinks, he made his way over to greet them. He was excited to meet Jack and honored to have him in his restaurant.

While Donnie and Mary were talking, Jack noticed his security guards were paying particular attention to a man in a charcoal suit with a black tie. The guards continued to keep their eye on the man, but relaxed a little as they ordered and were served a culinary work of art.

The first course consisted of a small salad with avocados, jalapenos, onions, diced yellow squash, and lettuce; all topped with a citrus dressing. Then, after the salad course, the staff served chicken and lime soup. It was extremely spicy, yet delicious. Finally, they were served the main course of steak and potatoes, which was also excellent.

As dinner was winding down, Donnie came back around to the table. He brought a complimentary desert wine he wanted them to try, and of course, nobody says no to Donnie.

Mary and Jack were enjoying the wine, when out of the corner of his eye, Jack saw both of his security guards jump to their feet. They made a move towards the man in

the charcoal suit, but he was already upon them. He had a
gun in his hand, and before Jack could even turn his head to
react, the man shot both the guards and turned the gun on
Jack and Mary.

Donnie, who was standing next to Mary, bent over and
wrapped his arms around her to shield her from gunfire.
The man kept coming and shot Donnie in the back. He
collapsed into Mary's arms and was bleeding profusely all
over her.

Jack reached down and grabbed a steak knife, jumped
up onto his chair, and leapt over the table to bring the
shooter down. They both fell to the floor, and Jack was able
to thrust the steak knife deep into his neck. But before he
had a chance to stab him again, the man hit him in the face
with the gun and knocked him back. Then he turned the
gun on Jack.

Suddenly, a shot rang out from behind the killer. One
of the guards had been able to pull himself up off the floor,
despite his wound, and killed the shooter before he could
kill Jack.

As he looked around to assess the carnage, Jack saw
Rick, the security guard that saved his life, attending to his
coworker who was obviously dead. The restaurant
employees were gathered together into small groups,
looking on in horror, and crying over the loss of their
beloved father and friend.

Donnie was still in Mary's lap and she was shaking
and crying hysterically. Jack went to her and gently laid
Donnie's body on the floor. Mary leaped into his arms,
weeping and kept repeating over and over, "Oh my God!
Oh my God! Oh my God!"

The police arrived quickly. Before it was over, there

were at least ten uniformed police officers on the scene, in addition to numerous detectives and crime scene specialists.

The police wanted to take Mary to the hospital, but she was hysterical and refused to go anywhere except back to the Hacienda with Jack. A police women took Mary into the bathroom and washed off as much of Donnie's blood as possible. She helped her out of her blood-soaked dress and into a dark green jumpsuit that one of the employees happen to have in her locker.

One of the Prince's contacts inside the police force called to tell him about the shooting and he rushed to the scene.

"Oh my God Jack, what happened?"

"This guy was having dinner one minute, and the next he was shooting us. It's like he was crazy."

The Prince walked over to where the body of the shooter was, and because he had worked so closely with the police over a long period of time, they allowed him watch as they examined the body.

The shooter lay dead on his back. His eyes were still open, blankly staring at the ceiling. A large chunk of his head was missing where Rick had shot him. His jacket had been ripped during his fight with Jack, and as the Prince looked closer, he could see part of a tattoo on his forearm and under his shirt. It was the Mark of the Feathered Serpent. It was an obvious forgery, and that explained why the shooter was acting like a man possessed. It was The Curse of the Feathered Serpent.

"You should come with me," said the Prince. "It's not safe for you to stay at the Hacienda any longer. I will move you all to my Penthouse. There are ample accommodations for everyone, and I can protect you there until we neutralize El Diablo."

As their driver took Jack and Mary to the Prince's penthouse, they rode without speaking. Jack was numb and Mary was curled up in his arms. When they got there, they went straight to the shower. They stood together under the flow of steam and hot water, and Jack held Mary tightly as she alternated between crying and a muted whimper.

Afterwards he helped her into bed and gave her a sleeping pill. Then he made himself a strong drink and sat on the couch in the bedroom so she wouldn't have to be alone.

Jack had a million questions swirling through his head, but there were two things he knew for sure. He was sure this was the work of El Diablo, and he was sure it wouldn't stop until he was neutralized.

Chapter 12

The Prince wanted everyone to move into his Penthouse in the morning. In the meantime, he insisted on leaving six security guards at the hotel that night.

Max stayed in Copan. He also had a date with Rosa that same night and was as excited as a teenager. At six-thirty, he knocked on her trailer door, right on schedule. When she answered it, Max could feel his heart melting. At that moment, she was the most beautiful woman in the world in his eyes.

They walked back to the Hacienda where Max had arranged for a van to pick them up. They rode to the landing zone, where the prince had a helicopter waiting to fly them to San Pedro Sula. They landed on the roof of the Prince's building, and were escorted to the elevators and down to the parking garage.

Even though the Prince was out on other business that night, his crew treated Max and Rosa like royalty.

When they got down to the Prince's private parking area, Max had a limo waiting. The driver took them to Le Café de Paris, a Five-Star gem specializing in French cuisine. It's one of San Pedro Sula's finest restaurants.

They were seated, and their security guards were seated at the next table. Max didn't think security was necessary, but the Prince insisted.

"Oh Max, this is a lovely place" Rosa said.

"Have you been here before?"

"No, I spend most of my time in Copan and I rarely come into the city. My work keeps me so busy."

The waiter came to the table and interrupted their conversation to serve the wine Max had ordered.

"How long have you been here?"

"I've only been here in Copan for the past three months. Before that I was in Palenque, excavating the tomb of Youl Ik Nal; the Red Queen."

"I didn't know that the Mayans had Queens."

"They didn't. She was the first and only woman ruler. She was the daughter of Pacal the Great. He was a powerful Mayan King who ruled Palenque for over thirty-years. Because he had no male heirs, his daughter ascended to the throne upon her father's death, an unheard of event in the Mayan world. She ruled for twenty-one years and was considered an excellent ruler. She led her people through a time of prosperity, and destroyed rival Kings who vied for her Kingdom. But in the end, she was betrayed by her lover and assassinated."

"What a sad story." Max said.

"When they found her tomb, they found her buried like a Queen. She was sealed in a hand-carved Limestone coffin in the heart of the temple on the main plaza of the city."

"You certainly love this stuff don't you Rosa?"

"Yes, it is true. I have always loved the study of Archeology, and especially the history of my own people, the Maya."

"How much longer will you be here?"

"Only another four to eight weeks, I believe. Whenever Dr. Nolan leaves, the whole team will go home with him."

"Do you mean Stacy's Uncle Robert?"

"Yes. He has been my teacher and mentor for so long I cannot call him anything but Dr. Nolan. He is truly an amazing man and one of the great Archeologists of our generation. I am grateful to be on his team, but I think we're all ready to go home."

"I think I'm ready to go too," Max said. "I'm ready to get back to Miami and back to the good old USA."

"Yes, I love living in Miami. I have a condo in Coral Gables" said Rosa.

"Isn't that funny?" said Max. "I live in Coconut Grove. We're practically neighbors."

"Good, then maybe we'll see each other again once we get back to Miami." said Rosa.

"I can guarantee it."

"That would be nice Max."

And as they enjoyed the fine French cuisine at Le Café de Paris, and the pleasure of each other's company, they became lost in the moment and the night flew by. Finally, after dinner was over they made their way back to the limo and straight back to the Prince's building.

As they rode home in the helicopter, they were holding hands and staring into each other's eyes like a couple of teenagers. And when he dropped her back off at her trailer, he took her in his arms and kissed her. Not a normal kiss. It was the kind of kiss a solider gives his girl when he comes home from war.

Max was in love, and the feeling was mutual.

Chapter 13

The whole group met in the restaurant at the Hacienda at 9:00 a.m. the next morning for breakfast. The Prince explained why he felt everyone should move into his Penthouse until they could eliminate El Diablo. They all agreed that it would be best, and made plans to pack up and move right after breakfast.

Max had arranged to meet Rosa at her trailer and to walk her over to the hotel, but when he knocked on her door there was no reply. He knocked several more times, but no one answered. He could see that all the lights were off, and no one was there, so he left. He was able to catch Stacy's Uncle in his trailer, but he hadn't heard from her either. So Max walked back to the hotel and rejoined the group.

"Where's Rosa?" Luke said.

"She wasn't in her trailer, and Stacy's Uncle Robert hadn't heard from her either." Max replied. "I tried calling her but she didn't answer."

"Well, let's give her a few minutes," Stacy said as the waitress began to pass out menus.

"I'm exhausted from yesterday, but it was the adventure of a lifetime and I'll never forget it," Mary said.

"That's for sure," Stacy added.

Then at once, Jack and Max got a look at Luke's tattoo and both let out a groan.

"Oh man, look at that thing," Max said. "The colors are incredible."

"I know," Luke agreed. "It's unbelievable. I've never seen anything like this before."

"Yeah," added Jack. "And just wait until your customers in Miami get a look at this. They'll be standing in line for one of these tattoos."

"I don't think so." Luke said.

"What do you mean?" Jack snapped back at him.

"You know it's not up to me. I can't do any tattoos yet without the supervision of the Shaman."

Jack looked mad and spoke to Luke in an angry tone.

"Well, that's all well and good, but I brought you down here to find the ink. And now that you've found it you're not going to give me any? I don't think so."

Luke could see that Jack was getting agitated, and he understood why. But now that his mind had been opened,

Luke understood why the ink must be guarded. It is a
sacred link between Kukulkan and his people. Only the
gods decide who will get a tattoo.

As we were squabbling over the ink the Prince got a
call. It was from Paco, his right hand man. He and the
Prince spoke for several minutes. After they hung up, the
Prince was momently silent; then he looked up at Luke and
spoke in a hushed tone,

"Have you seen the news?" he asked.

"No. Why?"

"There was another incident here in San Pedro Sula
this morning."

"What kind of incident?" Luke replied.

"Eyewitnesses say that two men got in an argument on
the street, and the next thing you know they started
fighting." The Prince continued, "They're saying that the
two men carried on beating one another until the man who
seemed to be getting the worst of it appeared to be dead."

"Oh my God!" Stacy blurted out. "Didn't anyone try to
help?"

"I guess not," said the Prince "because the TV reporter
said a crowd gathered, but nobody did anything."

"That's horrible," Mary said. "Did they arrest the
man?"

"I don't know. Paco said the police were still on the
scene and processing evidence."

Just then, Max returned to the table. He had excused
himself a few minutes earlier to get something he had left

in his hotel room. He had accidently left his TV on when he went to join the group for breakfast that morning, and when he went back to his room it was still on. The breaking news was on every channel. So when he sat back down at the table and heard what they were discussing he chirped right in.

"I just saw that on TV," Max said. "It's on every channel. It's all they're talking about."

"Did they catch the guy?" the Prince asked.

"No," Max answered. "They're saying he stole a car and drove it into a crowd of people eating breakfast on the plaza.

The Prince just sat there in silence trying to come to grips with what he was hearing as Max continued.

"They're saying he drove the car the length of the patio, than back onto the street. He jumped the curve and slammed into a building. The car hit the wall so hard it split into two pieces and exploded into a ball of fire. There were eight people dead, counting the killer, and another five injured, some of them critically."

"Do they know why he did it?" the Prince asked.

"No," said Max

"It sounds like the Curse," said the Prince

"Maybe it's time to go home." said Mary.

"I'm not going anywhere until I get some of that ink." said Jack.

"Stacy and I are going to stay at least another week." Luke agreed. "I need to finish my training with the

Shaman, and Stacy wants to spend some more time with her Uncle Robert."

"I wonder where Rosa is?" said Mary. "She's twenty-minutes late."

"I was just wondering the same thing myself," said Max as he picked up his cell phone and dialed Rosa's number again.

Rosa's phone rang two-three-four times before a man with a deep Latin voice answered. His voice was as cold as ice, and his tone made Max's skin crawl. It was the sound of pure evil.

"Who is this?" Max snapped.

"I am El Diablo."

"El Diablo!" Max said to himself.

There was a brief shuffling noise on the other end of the phone, and then Max heard Rosa's voice.

"Oh Max, help me."

"Rosa, where are you? Are you hurt?"

"No, not yet, but I'm afraid."

"Don't worry; I'll get you out of there."

"That's enough," said El Diablo. "Now I will do the talking. You will send Luke Taylor to me. He will tattoo the Mark of the Feathered Serpent on my arm. We will pick him up in one hour in front of the Hacienda San Lucas. Be ready. If you are not, I'll start sending Rosa back to you in pieces." Then he hung up.

Max hung up the phone and repeated El Diablo's

threat. At first no one spoke, and then the Prince took over.

"Ok. He wants the tattoo. But I think he'll kill Rosa either way."

"What can we do?" Jack said.

"I can tell you what I'm going to do," said Max. "I'm going to kill that son of a bitch."

"I'm with you Max," the Prince said. "But we must proceed carefully. He will kill Rosa's whole family without a thought to get what he wants."

"How do you know that they're there?" Jack said.

"He knows because he wears The Mark of the Hunter." Luke answered. "Kukulkan has told him, and I heard it too."

"We've been there." said Max. "They have a wraparound porch on the second floor that makes that place easy to defend."

"And the town is rich with potential victims," said the Prince, "So we must use caution."

"So what's your plan?" said Max.

"If Luke doesn't go with them in an hour, he'll hurt Rosa to get our attention, so Luke must go. The second floor allows fire superiority over any adversary who would approach the building. And with a heavy complement of security in the street, El Diablo will be hard to get to."

"So how do we get them out of there?' Max said.

"If we do a direct assault, he might kill Rosa and her family" the Prince said. "The only way to get them out of there alive is to totally neutralize the entire second floor."

When Luke arrives and begins the tattoo, he will activate gas bladders we will sew into his pants. They're very discrete, and won't be detected by El Diablo's men, even if he is frisked. The gas will totally disable everyone in the house, including Luke, Rosa, and her family. But it will cause them no permanent harm, and it will allow us to take out the thugs guarding the perimeter of the house before anyone on the inside has a chance to start shooting."

The Prince stepped away to make a call, and when he came back, he called the group together.

"I have called in my assault team. They will pick us up in the landing zone in forty minutes. We're taking fifteen men in two gunships. We're leaving four men here with Luke, Stacy, and Mary. Jose will take care of the gas bladders. The rest of us need to leave here in ten minutes. Jack, Max; go change."

Luke looked into Stacy's eyes and said "Are you okay with this?"

She looked straight back at him and said, "Do we have a choice?"

Chapter 14

The Prince used the hotel's van to carry himself, Jack, and Max out to the landing spot. When they arrived, the two helicopters and the Prince's assault team were waiting for them.

Jack, Max, and the Prince boarded one of the choppers. Once they were in and buckled up, their pilot turned around and flashed them a big smile. He reached out to shake hands with Jack and Max and said, "How ya' be? I'm Mike." Then he gave them a wink and a mischievous grin, pulled back on the throttle, and lifted the big bird slowly into the air. When they were safely off the ground, he lifted up the nose and soared off the into the morning sky like a man on a mission.

The Prince leaned over and whispered in Jack's ear, "This guy's a little bit of a cowboy, but he's a hell of a pilot."

Back at the Hacienda San Lucas, Jose finished sewing the gas bladders into Luke's pants. It was attached at his waistband, and ran down each leg. The bladder itself was made of latex, and would be difficult to detect. The bottom of each bladder had a tube that funneled the gas out between the bottoms of his pants and the tops of his shoes.

When he finished installing the gas bladders he showed Luke how to engage the trigger.

"Ok Luke, let me show you how this works." He began. "The mechanism is triggered from the switch in your pocket. It will trigger the gas bladders to dispense their cargo under extremely high pressure."

"Is the gas flammable?" Luke asked.

"Absolutely" Jose responded with a serious look on his face. "The gas is silent and has no smell, but it will overtake a medium-sized room in twenty-seconds or less. Also, when the trigger is hit, it will send an electronic signal that will tell the Prince when to attack.

At the appointed time, Luke stood in the hotel lobby waiting for his ride. He was nervous. He knew that once El Diablo had him, he would never let him go until he was done with him. Then he would probably kill him.

A black Hummer pulled up in front of the hotel. The rear door opened, and a man in military fatigues stepped out and motioned Luke over. He walked up to the vehicle and climbed into the back seat without a word. The man in military fatigues got back in the Hummer and slid into the seat next to him.

"Good morning, Mr. Taylor. El Diablo is looking forward to meeting you. He has heard that you have received the Mark of the McCaw, and I can see from your hand that it is true."

"What have you done with Rosa?" Luke demanded.

"She is fine. And as long as you cooperate she will not be harmed."

"*I don't believe a word the man says*" Luke thought to himself and spent the next two-hours riding to El Comino in silence.

As they entered the town, it appeared to be deserted. The townspeople had fled as soon as El Diablo's men arrived. Luke noticed two other black Hummers parked in front of the fabric shop that belonged to Rosa's parents. There were eight men roaming the street, and another four that he could see on the wrap around patio. They parked beside the other Hummers; and walked through the store, up the stairs, and into the family's residence.

As he stepped into the room, Luke's eyes were immediately drawn to the man sitting in the dining room at the head of the table. He stood when Luke entered the room. He was almost seven feet tall, with jet black hair that flowed below his shoulders. He had a full mustache and wore blue jeans with a wife beater t-shirt. His steel-toed boots looked more like weapons than shoes, and the prison tattoos that covered his body made him a terrifying sight.

He stepped over to where Luke was standing and stared down at him.

"I am El Diablo. I have sent for you. Give me your hand."

El Diablo took Luke's right hand and saw the Mark of the McCaw. Then he smiled.

"You will tattoo the Mark of the Feathered Serpent on one of my men. If you do it wrong and he should be cursed, my men will kill Rosa and her family. If you do it correctly, then you will tattoo me. And as long as you are doing it correctly; you, Rosa, and her family will be allowed to live. We will get started now."

El Diablo had created a tattoo station right there in Rosa's family's personal residence. He motioned for Luke to take a seat at the table and to lay out his tools.

As he did, he asked, "Where's Rosa and her family?"

"They are back in their bedrooms. But don't worry; they are safe and quite comfortable for now."

"I'm not going to start until I see Rosa," Luke said.

El Diablo became enraged and slapped Luke across the face so hard he almost knocked him out of his chair.

"You will do what you are told or you will die," he screamed.

Luke sat up in his chair and looked El Diablo straight in the eye.

There was an awkward silence as neither man spoke. Then without saying a word, he motioned for one of his men to bring out Rosa. The man went back to her bedroom, and walked her down the hall. When she saw Luke, she threw herself into his arms and wept.

Luke held her tightly and whispered in her ear, *"Hold on, help's coming."*

El Diablo grabbed Rosa and pulled her off of Luke, and then motioned for her to go back to her room and for Luke to get started on the tattoo.

Luke was sweating, and his breathing was coming in rapid gulps. His heart was beating out of his chest, and he could see El Diablo starting to look at him suspiciously. He knew that if the criminal found the gas bladders, or figured out that this was a trap, they were all dead. It was now or never, so he pressed the trigger switch and held his breath.

Luke could feel the gas pass over his ankles as the bladders silently emptied their toxic cargo into the room. Luke was determined to hold his breath for as long as possible, and it didn't take long before El Diablo's men started falling.

First, the man waiting to be tattooed fell out of his chair. Then the guard who went to see what was the matter with him also dropped to the floor, unconscious. There were three other guards in the room, and they were all knocked out within twenty-seconds.

Luke was still holding his breath, but was starting to get lightheaded. As he looked at El Diablo, he could see by the expression on the criminal's face that the he had figured out what was happening and made a dash for the patio and some fresh air. When he did, Luke picked up a rifle that one of El Diablo's thugs had dropped and bolted down the hall to the bedroom where Rosa and her family were being held. They were already unconscious, so Luke raised the window and allowed the clean air from outside the window to fill his lungs, but it was too late. The gas had done its job and Luke slumped over and fell into a nightstand that came crashing down on him.

When Luke had triggered the gas, the Prince had got the signal and moved into action. The two gunships that were sitting in a clearing five miles from El Comino rose and headed towards the fabric shop at top speed.

When they arrived on the scene, the men on the street still didn't realize what was going on upstairs because the gas was silent and almost all the victims had passed out without making a sound.

On the patio there were still four men unaffected by the gas, and El Diablo, who came running out of the house gasping for air.

The Prince tapped Mike on the shoulder and said "Would you keep those fellows in the street busy so I can land my team?"

"Aye, Captain," Mike responded as he pointed the big bird's nose down and started strafing the street below with the choppers big M-30 machine guns. El Diablo's terrified men ran for their lives while Mike turned around and made another pass at them. He was flying at less than twenty feet off the ground, and tearing up everything in his path, but he was careful not to hit the house where Rosa and her family were being held.

As he came back around for another pass, the other chopper was hovering over the house. They fired down on El Diablo and his four men on the patio; killing one, and forcing the other three, along with El Diablo, back into the house.

El Diablo and his men returned fire on the helicopter, and bullets pierced the choppers cabin. One of the Prince's men caught a bullet in the arm and began bleeding profusely. His blood was spilling all over the floor. One of his other men tried to stop the bleeding with a tourniquet as they continued firing down at El Diablo and his crew. Mike turned the chopper around, but was afraid to fire the M-30's directly on the building for fear of hurting Luke or Rosa. Meanwhile, the second chopper managed to keep El Diablo's thugs busy enough for Mike to land and unload the Prince and his men.

As soon as they hit the ground, the Prince and his team poured out of the chopper. As they did, a bullet found Max and hit him in the shoulder. He stumbled across the street and found cover behind the wall of a dilapidated three sided shed. He was trapped and was bleeding.

Jack and the Prince found cover and started returning fire on El Diablo's men when they realized that Max had been shot and was trapped behind the shed. One of the Prince's men made a move to get to him, but was shot almost as soon as he did.

"We've got to get him off the street or he's a dead man" said the Prince.

"Yeah" said Jack. "We need some kind of shield."

The Prince spotted a parked car at the end of the street and said to Jack "I've got an idea. If I can get that car started, I could drive it right down the middle of the street and pull him in."

"How are you going to get that car started without keys?" said Jack.

"I grew up on the streets of San Pedro Sula," the Prince responded with a grin. "This is not going to be the first time I hotwired a car."

In the meanwhile, Max was losing blood.

The Prince began working his way up the street towards the car, hiding behind walls. Jack continued firing on El Diablo's men to keep them distracted until the Prince could get there. When he finally reached the car, he was able to climb into the front by lying on the floorboard. He reached under the dash and hotwired the car. He got one hand on the brake and the other on the gear shifter and caused to car to lurch forward before it stalled. Quickly, he restarted the car, dropped it into drive, and pressed the gas pedal just enough to make the car start moving slowly down the street.

By now, several of the Prince's other men became aware of the situation and had come to help. They were able to drive El Diablo's men back just far enough to enable the Prince to reach Max. When he pulled up beside him, he was able to stop close enough for Max to crawl over to the car and climb into the back seat. Suddenly, another shot rang out and the Prince was hit in the arm. When Jack saw that, something snapped inside of him. He stood up and made a move towards the car without giving a thought to the danger that waited in the street.

He managed to reach the car without being shot, but

Max was weak from the loss of blood, and the Prince was unable to drop the transmission back into drive with his one good arm.

Jack climbed into the car and on top of the Prince as bullets continued to wiz by. He reached over and dropped the car into gear as the Prince pushed the gas pedal to the floor. The rear tires began to spin and throw dirt and gravel as the car shot down the street and off the road before it ran into a fence and came to a stop. All the while, the Prince's men continued to pour gunfire on El Diablo's crew as fast as possible and killed several of his thugs.

From his vantage point on the second floor, El Diablo could see that the second chopper had landed and the Prince's men would be upon him in a matter of moments. He knew it was over, so he and his three men from the patio climbed out a back window. They dropped to the ground below and were able to disappear without being detected. They ran two miles to a concealed road where El Diablo had left a Hummer waiting in case of an emergency. He and his men climbed in and drove off.

He had been forced to flee before they had a chance to hurt Rosa or her family. And the Prince's men were also able to round up another four of El Diablo's men from the street.

Two of the Prince's men had been killed, and four more wounded including Max and the Prince himself. Jack helped load the wounded into one of the choppers and dispatched it to the hospital in San Pedro Sula.

They ran into the building and upstairs into the residence to check on Luke, Rosa, and her family. They were all starting to regain consciousness, and when Rosa heard them she came running out of her bedroom.

"Thank God you're here," she said. She was still shaking and whimpering.

"At least it's all over now," Jack said.

But it wasn't.

El Diablo drove himself crazy thinking about the raid all the way home. He rode in silence for over an hour, then turned to the two thugs that had escaped with him and said "Luke has double-crossed me. I will make him my slave. The Prince and his friends have interfered in my business long enough. Now it's personal. Now they die. Now I will have their heads mounted on my wall like a trophy."

After Rosa's failed kidnapping attempt, EL Diablo was more determined than ever to get his hands on Luke. His rogue Shaman had failed to counterfeit the Mark of the Feathered Serpent, and every time he tried, the results were the same. The person being tattooed fell victim to the curse and went completely insane.

Back at his hideout, he plotted with his Shaman to capture Luke, and to kill the others.

"Luke is protected by Kukulcan" the Shaman said. "Soon he will have the power to defeat you. He must be eliminated now."

"That's not easy to do." El Diablo said. "He's constantly being protected by the Prince and his people."

"Yes." said the Shaman. "And Kukulcan has placed a wall of protection around him." Nobody can get to him through mortal power. The only way to defeat Luke will be to reach into the pit of hell and call upon the power of Ah Puch, the Lord of Death."

"Can you do that?"

"I can. But once I do, there will be no going back."

"What do you mean *"there's no going back?"*"

"I will tattoo the Mark of the Skull on your shoulder. Once it's in place, you will be empowered, but your soul will belong to Ah Puch. Once you sell your soul to the Lord of Darkness, there is no going back."

"Well, if he takes me to hell, I expect a lot of my friend's will be there too." said El Diablo with a grin. "Besides that, I'm probably going to hell anyway."

"You would do well to show respect." said the Shaman. "Ah Puch smites those who displease him, and destroys all those who will not bow to his will."

"How powerful will I be?" El Diablo wondered out loud.

"You will have the power to control men's minds. They will hear your voice in their heads and bend to your will. You will bring down fire from the heavens, and you will have power over matter, so that you can move objects at will."

"I could use mind control on the police, the military and maybe even government officials." El Diablo thought to himself. "Where will we find Ah Puch?"

"Where the Xalbal River flows through the holy mountain, there you will find the entrance to the underworld of the dead" the Shaman said.

Two days later, El Diablo and his Shaman found themselves high in the mountain jungles of Guatemala. They were in a boat on the Xalbal River at the Caves of Candelaria. In several places the river rapids were daunting, and it was all they could do to stay in the boat and avoid river rocks. They did find several caves, but they all turned out to be nothing.

Suddenly the river rapids calmed down, and the boat glided gently through the water. The Shaman spotted a small fork in the river and took it. They both had tingles of anticipation wondering what awaited them around the corner, and they both were amazed at what they saw.

The river flowed directly into a cave and through the mountain.

"The Pupol Vuh speaks of the sacred river that flows through the mountain" said the Shaman. There you will find the entrance to the underworld of the dead, and there is where we will call on Ah Puch, the Lord of Darkness."

The entrance was more massive then they had expected. They entered the cave and traveled by boat at least a hundred yards through the pitch black underground river. They carried torches to light their way through the darkness until they finally came to the chamber of Xibalba. They stepped out of the boat and pulled it out of the water and onto the stone floor. The Shaman positioned torches to provide light, and strategically placed incense burners to allow the room to fill with smoke quickly.

The Shaman sat on the stone floor and instructed El Diablo to do the same. Then he began to chant Mayan prayers with an increasingly demanding tone. EL Diablo raised his eyes towards the heavens, and started chanting the same Mayan prayers. The Shaman began to pick-up the pace and intensity until he was almost screaming for the Dark Angel to show himself.

Gradually, the room began to get cold, and kept getting colder and colder until it was cold enough to see your breath. The stone floor was damp and frigid, and El Diablo noted that no living thing could exist in this place. It was void of all life.

They began to become aware of a smell that was filling the chamber. It was a vile stench, like dead rotting flesh. The smell continued to grow stronger, and as it did, it became more and more pungent until they didn't think they could stand it another second.

"What is this?" El Diablo said.

"Be Silent. It is the smell of death" the Shaman said as he continued to chant Mayan prayers and call out to Ah Puch to show himself.

The sound of tiny tinkling bells and rattling bones could be heard as Au Puch slowly began to materialize before their very eyes. His body was a skeleton with the head of an owl, and his eyeballs hung on nerves to the middle of his chest. There were tiny bells tied to his head feathers that tinkled as he moved calling the guilty to hell. He carried a leather satchel which held the souls of his victims. The sound of wailing and gnashing of teeth could clearly be heard as the dammed called out for mercy. But there would be no mercy, and the more they cried out, the happier it seemed to make Ah Puch.

Maybe for the first time in his life, El Diablo was scared. Then the Shaman spoke.

"Mighty Lord, we call on your name. Hear our prayer and see the soul of this man who has come here to be transformed. Empower him with evil as he does your will. Strengthen him and shield him as he destroys your enemies."

Ah Puch made no sound, but nodded his acceptance of the deal. Slowly he moved towards El Diablo with his bones rattling and the bells in his hair tinkling. The foul smell continued to get worse, and when the Lord of Death touched him on the shoulder, it burned like he was being hit with a branding iron. The outline of the skull appeared, and Ah Puch motioned for the Shaman to complete the tattoo by adding the color.

When it was over, El Diablo was sure that he heard laughter as Ah Puch slowly faded away. As he did, the smell receded and the chamber began to warm up to its normal temperature.

El Diablo continued to sit in silence with his eyes closed. His arm was hurting from the tattoo he just received, and he was in shock from the whole experience, but he was anxious to test out his new powers.

"How is it that I have power over matter? What does it mean and how do I use it?"

"You can move objects at will. You can make them crash or burst into a fireball."

The only things in the room to move were the Shaman's tattoo bag and the boat they had come in.

"Just concentrate on the tattoo bag and will it to rise off the ground."

So El Diablo did just that, and the tattoo bag slowly rose several feet off the ground.

As he did, the boat they had come in lifted up off the ground and made a complete circle around the room. It made several passes before it stopped and gently landed right back where it started.

The Shaman sat and observed the boat.

"You have power over matter" he said.

The room was still dark except for the torchlight that the Shaman had set up, and the only sound was the gentle flow of water from the river that ran through it. But the silence was interrupted when an energy source began to take form in the far corner of the chamber. It continued to take shape and grow in size and intensity until El Diablo willed it to strike, then it shot out of the corner like a bullet from a gun, and crashed into the river where it was extinguished before anyone was hurt.

This time, even El Diablo was startled by the fireball. He opened his eyes just in time to see the ripples and the smoke rising out of the water where it hit. Then he looked to the Shaman and said "How do I control men's minds?"

"Be silent. Be still. Focus on them until you can hear what they're thinking, and then tell them what to think and do. They will think that your thoughts are their thoughts. Transmit your spirit through space until you are close enough to see them and for them to see you" the Shaman said.

So El Diablo began to think about Luke.

Chapter 16

After the raid to rescue Rosa, Stacy and Luke moved into the Prince's personal residence along with the others. Once El Diablo knew they were at the Hacienda they weren't safe there anymore. It was too difficult to protect them there, and it also presented an unreasonable risk to the other guests of the hotel, so the Prince had the whole group moved for their protection.

Luke was more determined than ever to stop El Diablo before he could strike again. That thug would resort to anything to get to him, and he had to be dealt with before they could focus on doing the things we came down here for.

Max was admitted to the hospital. His wound was not too serious, but he had lost a lot of blood and needed to stay overnight.

The Prince had taken a bullet in the arm, but the

wound wasn't too bad either. He was treated and released.

The next morning they reviewed their plans at breakfast.

"Stacy and I are staying in Honduras for at least another week." Luke said. "I'm going to finish my training with the Shaman, and Stacy wants to spend a little more time with her Uncle." But as he spoke, he couldn't fight the feeling that someone was standing over his shoulder. It felt like someone was watching him.

"We need to go home for a while." Jack said. "The Dolphin's first mini-camp starts in other two-weeks and I need some time to get my head in the game."

"But we're coming back." Mary said. "We've fallen in love with the Mayan children and we're coming back to work with the Prince to help them."

"I'm also hoping to get a tattoo with that ink" Jack added.

"I'm going to hang around for another week or so" Max said. "Rosa's still trying to recover from the trauma of the last two days. In the meantime, I can continue running Jack's affairs from the Penthouse."

Later that evening, after Stacy and Luke had a chance to rest, they met with the rest of the group to have a farewell dinner for Jack and Mary. They dined in the Prince's elegant dining room amidst his gallery of precious artwork and ancient artifacts. Everyone was there, and there was a festive atmosphere in the room as they recounted the events of the last two weeks.

After dinner, they sat and talked, enjoying fine wines and liquors. Nobody paid much attention to the man who came in and walked over to the Prince. The man handed the Prince a letter, then leaned down and whispered something in his ear. The Prince read the letter, and as he did, his face turned white as ash. Tears began to well up in his eyes. He hung his head, and was unable to speak. It was unbelievable to see him this way.

Finally, he gained control of himself. He handed Luke the letter, and began to speak.

"San Luis is gone."

"That's the village we visited," said Mary.

"What do you mean it's gone?" Jack said.

"El Diablo has destroyed the entire village. He burned down the storehouse, the dormitory and all the houses we built. He has destroyed everything. He killed every man, woman, and child. He even killed the animals. It's all gone. Here, Luke, read the letter."

Luke's voice was shaking as I read the letter out loud.

"Your friends in San Luis are no more. They were killed because you have defied me. You will bring Luke back to Copan. He will call 555-2454-1211. I will tell him where to go. If you do not obey, I will destroy another village, and continue to destroy villages until you submit to my will. The longer you wait, the more innocent people will die."

Mary screamed and burst into tears, as did Stacy and Rosa. Jack, Max and Luke were shocked and speechless. The enormity of the massacre was hard to comprehend. The Prince was numb at first, and then he got angry.

"I am going to kill him" said the Prince. "Tomorrow

we're going to San Luis at sunrise. I must see for myself. If it is true, and I believe that it is, then the Mayans living throughout the mountains are in grave danger. We need to notify the Council of Elders and the Military." He turned to the man who had brought the letter and instructed him to call the Army Base at San Pedro Sula and have the Colonel notified of the situation.

Shortly after that, the Prince got a call on his personal line. It was Colonel Morales. They spoke for several minutes as the Prince updated him on the situation.

After he hung up the Prince said, "Tomorrow morning the Colonel is sending a squad up to check it out."

"Stacy and I are going too," Luke said, "and I'll let the Shaman know what happened."

"So are we," said Jack, who tried to comfort Mary. The thought of all those poor little souls dying such a terrible death was almost more than Mary could take.

"I'm sorry Luke," Rosa said, "but I can't bear to see such a sight."

"It's ok," Luke replied. "It's probably better that you don't go. You've been through a lot with the kidnapping and everything."

"I'll stay here with Rosa," Max said.

"That's a good idea" said Jack. You need to give that wound a chance to heal. Then everyone excused themselves and retired to their quarters. It seems that after the news about San Louis, nobody felt much like celebrating.

The next morning, they headed out at sunrise.

Unfortunately, there's no way to get to San Louis by air, so they were forced to drive. As they made their way over mountain roads and thick jungle foliage Luke was taken aback again and again by how beautiful Honduras is.

It took every bit of two hours to get to San Luis, and when they arrived they were horrified. Every building in the village had been completely destroyed. The bodies of villagers were strewn around the village square and down paths that led to homes. Inside the rubble of the buildings were the burned bodies of El Diablo's victims. The children had been rounded up and executed in the town square. Their lifeless bodies were piled on top of one another, and Luke were sure that this must be the most horrific sight ever seen by human eyes.

As they waded through the rubble, no words were spoken. The silence was only interrupted by the sounds of the jungle. When Mary saw the bodies of the children who had been executed, she fell to her knees and sobbed, "How could anyone do such a thing?"

"We are dealing with pure evil," the Prince said. "He kills without remorse and never looks back. No one is safe until this mad man is gone. He will never let himself be taken alive. But I will find him. And when I do, I will give him a message from the children of San Louis."

On the ride back to Copan the Prince sat in silence for the first twenty-minutes, and then he spoke to the group.

"We're going to have to eliminate El Diablo once and for all. I cannot allow him to continue killing innocent women and children to get at us. Sometimes he can be found playing cards in the Social Room, on the second floor of a bar in San Pedro Sula. I'm going to pay him a visit as soon as I'm sure he's there. He's going to disappear and never be heard from again."

Chapter 17

Luke was with the Prince in his office. Jack was there and together they were making plans for the raid on El Diablo's hangout on the second floor of Rico's Cantina.

"I've got a man watching the building who will let me know when he shows up" the Prince said. "Pete has been there for almost a week and he thinks that El Diablo will be there later today. When he does show up, I can mobilize ten men in fifteen-minutes and we'll pay him a little visit."

"Why do you go on these raids yourself?" Jack said.

"I don't go on all of them, but this one's important. My presence will be a great advantage to my men. I also want to make sure we catch that animal. I have a message for him from the children of San Luis, and I want to look into his eyes as I give it to him."

The Prince ordered lunch, but just as they were getting

served he got a call from Pete, his lookout at Rico's Cantina. El Diablo was there.

The Prince stood up and said, "Are you ready to go?"

"I'm ready," Luke said.

"So am I," said Jack.

The Prince made a call to his assault team, and they assembled in the parking garage. Discretion would be important. They needed to get there without being detected by El Diablo's men, so the Prince had his attendant bring around three inconspicuous sedans, and they reviewed the plan one more time before they left

"El Diablo and his men are playing cards upstairs in the Social Club," said the Prince. "There are only two ways in and out of that room. There's a covered staircase with doors on both ends that leads into the parking lot at the bottom, and the Social Club at the top. I am going to lead you five up the stairs and into the room. In the meantime, Carlos is going to lead the rest of you up the stairs in the back of the bar that lead up to the Club. If we can catch them in a cross fire, we can end it before they know what hit them. The key will be speed. And remember, our main job today is to take out El Diablo himself. If you get a shot at him, take it. Once he's been put down, withdraw and we can go home. We don't need to kill everyone, just him."

When they got there they parked the cars behind the club. The men quickly gathered around the Prince for any last minute instructions.

"We've got to get in there fast. Once the shooting starts, the police will respond within five to ten minutes. El Diablo has plenty of them on his payroll, so we need to be gone before they get here. Remember, any of El Diablo's men would kill you if he got the chance, so show no mercy. But don't forget, our main goal is to take out El Diablo himself. Once he's confirmed dead, back out."

Jack and Luke, along with the rest of his team made their way around to the front of the building. They walked into the bar and straight back to the staircase without making eye contact with anyone. They expected to find one or two of El Diablo's men guarding the stairs to the Social Club, but there was nobody, so they made their way up the stairs and waited for the signal to go in.

The Prince opened the back door and started up the dark staircase. Again, there was nobody guarding the stairs, and the Prince became suspicious. When he got to the top, he made sure his crew was ready and then burst through the doorway. He did a roll and ended up back on his feet with his rifle raised and ready to fire, but he hesitated. His men had run up the stairs after him, but stopped short when they entered the room.

The Social Club was empty. There was nobody there but poor Pete. El Diablo had used his ability to control men's mind's to plant the idea in Pete's head that the criminal would be there, but it was a trap. El Diablo's men tortured him for information on the Prince and Luke. And once he outlived his usefulness, they hanged Pete and left his lifeless body dangling by a rope from the ceiling as a warning.

The crew that came up through the bar bolted through the other door at almost the exact same moment, but they also stopped short when they saw that the room was empty.

"What the hell!" Jack exclaimed.

"It's an ambush," said the Prince. "El Diablo's men turned the tables on us."

They were trapped in a room with very little cover and bad guys coming up the stairs on both sides.

The Prince had to think fast. The only furniture in the room was a large round card table with heavy wooden chairs that we could use to block one of the doors.

Just then, the door leading to the parking lot opened and several of El Diablo's men burst through, firing randomly into the room. One of the Prince's men was killed and another badly wounded before they turned their guns on the doorway and returned fire, killing two of El Diablo's men and driving a third back into the stairwell.

The Prince turned around and pulled the table over onto the floor. He started to drag it toward the door that led to the bar just as El Diablo's men were coming up the stairs.

His men were been able to drive El Diablo's thugs back down the stairs long enough to drag the table over and use it to block the door.

The Prince knew he needed to get out of the room and into the parking lot before the rest of El Diablo's crew were able to get back around the building. If they did, his men would have a harder time getting to their cars for an escape.

He picked up a heavy wooden chair from the card table and started down the stairs, using the chair like a shield against enemy fire. Because he had been wounded rescuing Rosa, he couldn't hold a gun and the chair at the same time, so two of his men followed him down the stairs shooting over his shoulder.

Three of his men were dead and four more were wounded. Two of the wounded were able to get out on their own, but the other two were not, and if they wanted to make it out of there alive they needed to do it now.

Jack ran over to help one of the Prince's men who had been seriously wounded. He picked him up and threw him over his shoulder, then ran to the stairs where the other wounded man was struggling to get up. Jack helped him to his feet and down the stairs; while all the way down he carried the Prince's other man on his shoulder.

The Prince made it to the bottom of the stairs using the chair as a shield. He had two men that had not been shot, and two more that were wounded and struggling to keep up. There were still three of the Prince's men who lay dead in the Social Room, but he was unable to do anything for them now.

The Prince burst through the door and into the parking lot. There were four of El Diablo's men in the parking lot firing at him from behind parked cars. There was a fifty-foot space between the Prince and the shooters. He bolted out the door using the chair as a shield while his other two men continued to fire back at El Diablo's thugs. He slid over the hood of a car with the chair still in hand like a shield, but now he used it as a weapon to disable one of El Diablo's men. The man dropped his weapon as he fell. Jack used his good hand to pick it up and kill one of the men who had been shooting at him, while his other two men took care of the other three men who had been shooting at them as well.

Jack followed the Prince down the stairs still carrying one of the wounded on his shoulder, and helping the other man stay on his feet enough to limp to the car. About that same time, the Prince and the other men who were still alive managed to reach the sedans and get in as they raced out of the parking lot. El Diablo's men continued to fire as they drove away, but they didn't pursue them, and the

Prince drove his wounded men directly to the hospital.

Chapter 18

The next morning El Diablo enjoyed a full breakfast. He and his inner circle had been up late the night before celebrating their victory. The Prince and his men had taken a terrible beating at their hands, and they would revel in it.

El Diablo's rogue Shaman was busy tattooing his thugs, but all the men who received the counterfeit Feathered Serpent tattoo fell victim to the Curse and went insane. The first one killed a waitress and five patrons in a restaurant. The second one killed several pedestrians before he drove a car into a crowd eating breakfast on the plaza. And the third one tried to kill Jack and Mary at Donnie's Restaurant.

After that, none of El Diablo's men would agree to being tattooed, so they began plucking innocent victims off the street and let the Shaman give them the counterfeit tattoos. He was hopeful that given enough time, his

Shaman would get it right.

El Diablo had built a fire pit based on the Shaman's recollection of the one in the ceremonial chamber. They had carved out stone bowls and chiseled out the stone rods from solid rock. His men had scoured the jungle collecting flowers and clay for the ink. But there was still something missing.

It was the water.

At least that's what El Diablo's Shaman said. He had been making ink since he was a boy, and had made it hundreds of times. His arrogance led him to believe he could tattoo the Mark of the Feathered Serpent without the Temple water and without the hand of Kukulkan. But no matter what he used, he couldn't make it work. Even after they managed to steal Temple water, it still didn't work.

El Diablo was skeptical. He was starting to believe that the Shaman had lost his power, but he could still be useful. He could use The Curse to his benefit. He could create homicidal maniacs and send them out to do things that were so terrible, even his own men wouldn't do them. Things like the massacre at San Luis. He would use this to force Luke's hand, and now was the time to strike, while the Prince was weak.

El Diablo's thugs plucked four hapless victims off the street, and his Shaman gave them each the counterfeit Feathered Serpent tattoo. Within a few hours, their minds began to deteriorate and they went insane. They were extremely irritable and were barely able to be in the same room with one another for more than a minute or two. However, when set out upon a common task, they suddenly began to work like a team.

They were highly susceptible to the Shaman's

suggestions, and when he used his mind control, he was able to send them to La Paz with instructions to destroy everyone and everything.

They loaded up the Hummer with rifles, shotguns, and ammunition for the trip. They also took a large supply of small explosive devices as well as accelerants that could be used to create fires. Each one was equipped with everything from pistols to brass knuckles. And they took several bottles of liquor for the trip, which they consumed enroute.

When they got to La Paz they pulled into the center of the village. The children ran out to greet them, as well as several elders. The murderer's climbed out of the Hummer and walked around to the back of the vehicle. They reached in to retrieve rifles. They calmly loaded the weapons and walked back around to the front of the vehicle and began to shoot, randomly picking their victims. They separated, and methodically walked through the village in an attempt to be as thorough as possible.

A few of the adults and some of the children were able to escape into the jungle. But danger lies around every corner in the mountain jungles of Western Honduras, and they would be defenseless against predators.

After several sweeps of the village, the killers were satisfied that there was no one left alive. They killed the livestock: the pigs, the goats, and the chickens the villagers depended on for food. They set the village on fire, as they strategically placed the accelerant to burn as rapidly as possible.

Once the massacre was complete, the four murderers began to squabble among themselves. El Diablo was able to control their mind, even from a hundred miles away. Eventually he let them kill each other, and the last man standing put a shotgun in his own mouth and pulled the trigger.

Later that day, some of the villagers that escaped into the jungle were able to get help from a neighboring village and return, but there was very little to return to. There was no food or shelter. It was almost as if the village had never existed.

When the Prince got word of the massacre at La Paz he slumped down in his chair, put his head in his hands, and wept. Then almost immediately, his countenance changed from sorrow to rage. He made a phone call and walked out of his office.

Luke was working with the Shaman in the Temple that day when Kukulkan spoke to his spirit. He stopped what he was doing and stood in silence. The Shaman did the same. After a few minutes, he opened his eyes and turned to the Shaman and said, "I must go to La Paz."

"I know," the Shaman said. You are ready. Let me make sure you take the supplies you will need. Did Kukulkan tell you what kind of tattoos you will do?"

"It will be the Butterfly of Life," Luke responded.

So the Shaman made sure Luke had the inks and needles he would need, and sent him off.

Luke had been escorted to the Temple by four body guards earlier that morning. The Prince had insisted it was necessary for his protection, so they all climbed back into the Range Rover and set off for La Paz.

The Prince and his men were already there when Luke arrived, and were stepping around the bodies looking for survivors. The death toll was staggering. There were at least forty adults and another twenty or so children, all dead.

When Luke got out of the vehicle he paused as Kukulkan spoke to his spirit, and then he walked around to the back of the charred remains of the storehouse. He found a young girl who looked to be about five or six. She had been seriously wounded, but was still alive. He carried her around to the front of the building and had someone make a place to lay her down.

They dressed her wound and gave her water. Then Luke began to tattoo her with the Butterfly of Life. They maintained pressure on the wound until he could finish the tattoo. It took over an hour; and then gradually, as Luke was doing the tattoo, the bleeding slowed down until it stopped altogether. As they cleaned the wound they found that the bullet hole had closed up, and there was no sign of a bullet wound whatsoever. Luke looked up at the Prince who had been assisting him but neither one of them said a word.

While Luke was doing the tattoo, one of the Prince's men called out that he had found another survivor. And then there were two more. Luke feared that some would die before he could get to them. But just as he was starting the second tattoo, another truck pulled into the village. A man got out, and the first thing Luke noticed was that he had the Mark of the McCaw, the sign of the Tattoo Master, tattooed on his right hand. The Prince approached the man, and they spoke a few words in Spanish. Then the man simply found the next victim and began the Butterfly of Life tattoo.

Soon after, another Master of Tattoo came into the village on horseback. He dismounted and found his way to the next wounded villager.

All in all they found seven survivors that they were able to save with tattoos. They would call the Army in to remove the bodies. But after the massacre at San Luis, and now this, Luke knew that we had to find a way to stop El Diablo now.

He found the Prince and walked him over to where the killers had been fighting amongst themselves and he showed him their tattoos. It was the Mark of the Feathered Serpent. The rogue Shaman had tattooed these four and brought on the Curse. Then the Prince showed Luke the letter that he had received from El Diablo.

"La Paz is no more. They were killed because you have defied me. You will bring Luke back to San Pedro Sula. He will call 555-2454-1211. I will tell him where to wait. If you do not obey, I will destroy another village, and continue to destroy villages until you submit to my will. The longer you wait, the more innocent people will die."

Luke knew he had a serious problem. El Diablo had to be stopped, but how? He was hard to find because he had begun moving his operation around to avoid detection, never staying in one spot more than a week or two.

The other issue was the fact that there was simply too large an area to patrol. There were literally hundreds of small villages carved out of the jungle and scattered throughout the mountains. El Diablo was going to be hard to stop because there was no way to monitor the whole area at once, and it was impossible to predict where he would strike next.

The Prince visited Colonel Morales at the Honduran Army Base in San Pedro Sula. When he heard about the massacres, the Colonel became enraged and agreed with the Prince - they needed to find El Diablo before he had a chance to strike again.

They developed a plan to have the Army begin aerial scans over the jungle in the hope of stumbling across El Diablo's hideout. In the meantime, the Prince would work the streets looking for anyone who knew anything about his whereabouts. Every man has his price, and the Prince's men began a systematic process of tracking down El Diablo's known associates. They were betting that they could find someone who would be willing to sell him out for money.

The Prince needed El Diablo neutralized quickly. The constant battle was taking a toll on his business. He had lost eleven men to El Diablo in the last month. These were good men who could not be easily replaced. He had also lost several important clients because he didn't have the resources available to do the job. They were too busy making raids on El Diablo.

Early the next morning, Luke returned to the Temple of Kukulkan to continue his tattoo training. Dario was there to assist as Luke made the ink for the day's tattoo, and he was careful not to drop the red hot stone bowls as he lifted them off the fire.

After the paste had a chance to cool, Luke carried a bucket over to the crystal clear stream that flowed under the Temple and filled it. As he poured the water into the stone bowls, the paste gradually turned into ink, and the colors came alive.

Once the ink was ready, they sat on their mats in

silence and waited for the Shaman to arrive. As he entered the room they both stood up. The Shaman greeted each of them and instructed them to be seated. Luke was anxious to tell the Shaman about the massacre at San Louis, but he already knew about it.

"El Diablo has killed the people of San Louis and La Paz, and he will continue to hurt the innocent until he gets to you" the Shaman said.

"Yes" Luke agreed. "He believes that he can receive the Mark of the Feathered Serpent without the blessing of Kukulcan."

"And now you face another danger. He has sold his soul to Ah Puch, the Dark Angel; and has become powerful enough to destroy you. He must be dealt with. It is time for you to receive the Mark of the Feathered Serpent. The Mayan Council of Elders is prepared to receive you at dawn, here in the Temple."

When he was finished speaking the Shaman lifted his hands towards the heavens and began chanting Mayan prayers. He continued, getting more intense as he went along. As he prayed, heaviness descended on the room, and the presence of Kukulkan filled the place. Luke's mind was opened, and in his spirit he heard the voice of the War Serpent. He told Luke things that were yet to come, and although he didn't understand all of it yet, he understood that the situation was serious and that he was going on a journey.

After a time the presence of Kukulkan began to fade and the room returned to normal.

Later that night, back at the Prince's Penthouse, Stacy and Luke lay in bed with eyes wide open. *"What's waiting for me in the morning?"* he wondered. He didn't know, and the anticipation was making it hard to sleep. Ever since they'd been in Honduras they had heard of the Mark of the Feathered Serpent, and yet, they hadn't actually seen a real one ... yet.

When the morning sun finally arrived, Luke felt as if he had been wide awake all night, but at some point he must have fallen asleep because the alarm startled him when it went off.

He got up and stumbled to the bathroom. Stacy groaned and pulled a pillow over her head. She would wait in the relative safety of the Prince's Penthouse until he returned.

His mind was racing as he jumped into the shower and got dressed. *"What were they going to do to me?"* he thought. He could only imagine, but the anticipation of the unknown was making him very excited and nervous all at the same time.

After he was dressed he took the elevator to the top floor. The Prince had arranged to have a helicopter fly him to Copan, and when he got up there the chopper was waiting for him.

"This is a very big deal" said the Prince.

"I know" Luke said.

"Did they say how long you'll be gone?" the Prince asked.

"No. Kukulcan told me I was going on a journey, but he didn't say where I'm going or how long I'll be away" Luke said.

"Well, we'll see" said the Prince. "In the meantime, I'll watch over Stacy until you get back."

"Thank you Juan" Luke said as he looked him in the eye and shook his hand.

Mike was flying the chopper that day, and when Luke climbed in Mike could see that he was nervous. He turned around and gave Luke a grin and said "How ya be? Big doin's today?"

"It looks like it" Luke replied. And as Mike took them out and over the dense jungle below, Luke kept asking himself "*What am I getting into?*"

The chopper landed in the usual place, and the Prince had arranged for a van to take Luke to the ruins and the Temple of Kukulcan.

"They landed in the clearing, and Luke took the van that was waiting for him into Copan and the Temple. When he arrived, he found his way around to the back entrance that led him through the tunnels and into the ceremonial chamber. It was the same room where all his previous training had taken place, and he was starting to believe that he belonged there.

Inside the room there were five Shamans who he assumed were the Council of Elders. Each Shaman had an apprentice. Luke recognized Dario as one of the group, and after everyone was seated, he began to serve the Yage tea. It was the same tea he had tried at Rosa's parent's house. He remembered what an effect it had on him then, so he was nervous about trying it again. But by now, Luke's hunger to understand the power of the ink, and how to use it, far outweighed his fear of the unknown.

When he drank the tea he became sick to his stomach almost immediately. Fortunately, he found the bucket that Dario had placed next to his mat for this very purpose. He managed to keep his mess from touching the chamber floor, which was important because the Shaman had instilled in Luke a reverence for this holy place.

The effect of the tea was similar to the first time. The room became electric. There was a loud buzz in his head like an old florescent light bulb on its last legs. Neon colors flashed all around him, and his mind was racing. Still, Luke felt calmness unlike anything he had ever experienced.

One of the Shamans produced a knife. It was made of razor sharp obsidian and its handle was bejeweled with jade. He sliced the palm of his hand, deep enough to draw blood, but not sufficient to require stiches. He allowed the blood droppings to fall into a small pile of very thin bark and leaves as he passed the knife to the next Shaman, who did the same. As the Shamans passed the knife from one to another, each cut his hand and allowed the blood to drip onto the pile of leaves.

The knife was passed to Luke, but he was instructed not to use it on himself. Rather, he was told to pass it on to the next Shaman.

After the circle was complete, they lit the pile and ingested the smoke as it rose from the fire. The blood offering still has deep spiritual meaning to the K'iche' Maya.

They all prayed intently until heaviness fell on the chamber, and the War Serpent made his presence felt. Luke tried to sit up straight but was unable to move. The

Shamans all continued praying at once, and called on Kukulcan to give them wisdom.

As Luke ingested the smoke, his mind was opened. Kukulkan spoke to his spirit and prepared him for a journey. He understood that the only way to stop El Diablo was to take the Mark of the Feathered Serpent and to physically beat him.

After the prayers died down, one of the Elders looked at Luke and said "The Mark of the Feathered Serpent is the sacred tattoo of the Warrior Healer. The one who carries the Mark will be empowered with the speed and strength of the jaguar. His reflexes are razor sharp and his eyes see clearly, even at night."

"And he dedicates his life to protecting the Mayan people" said another.

"But he is also a healer" one of the other Shaman interjected. "He lives and works among the people, and uses the tattoos to heal and protect those whom Kukulcan has chosen."

"Kukulcan said my wife would be tattooed. What does that mean?"

"Your wife is to receive the Mark of K'Na, the patroness of wisdom and knowledge. She will be your partner and open your eyes. She will know things before they happen. Listen to her. Kukulcan will give her great wisdom and strength. And together you will do the work Kukulcan has called you to do.

"Who's going to do her tattoo?" Luke asked.

"She will receive the Mark of K'Na here in the temple of Kukulcan tomorrow."

"What about me?"

"To get the Mark of the Feathered Serpent, you must make your way to the lost city of El Mirador and the temple of the Jaguar. There you will seek the blessing of the Ancient Mayan King *Great Fiery Jaguar Paw*. Mayan warriors have made this journey for over a thousand years to receive the anointing of the King who is a god."

"When will I leave and who will take me" Luke wondered out loud.

"Your journey begins here and now. You will go directly from here to the landing strip. You will be flown to Flores, where you will meet Tomas, your guide. He will help you get the supplies you will need for the journey."

"How will I find this city? Is there a map?"

"There is a map, but it's only a rough guide. Very few people have ever been there, and the trip is fraught with danger."

"If the jungle doesn't kill you the looters might" added one of the Shamans.

"I thought that a Shaman or a Master of Tattoo could do the tattoo with the blessing of Kukulcan."

"Yes, but to defeat El Diablo you must have the power to transform. Only then can you keep him from controlling your mind. You must seek out the spirit of the Jaguar King. There you will receive the tattoo."

And with that ominous thought they helped Luke gather up his things and prepare to leave. They had prepared sufficient ink for numerous tattoos, and packed his satchel with tattoo needles and the other instruments that he would need to do tattoos out in the world.

The Council members embraced Luke as he left the chamber, and Dario escorted him to the van which drove him to the airstrip. The plane was waiting for him when he got there, and as soon as he was on board it taxied to the end of the runway and prepared for takeoff.

Luke had flown in large commercial jets on numerous occasions, but going up in one of these small single propeller airplanes was a daunting experience and he tried very hard not to look down.

He felt different. Uneasy. Something was happening. He was gradually changing; both his thoughts and feelings were becoming more focused on the power of the tattoos, and what he could do to help others. Kukulkan had spoken to his spirit, and guided his hand. Yes, things were different, and he felt empowered.

"Perhaps I could use my gifts to help the Mayan people living in the mountain villages." he thought. *"Most of them don't have adequate medical care. Perhaps that is what I've has been called here to do."*

He had a lot of questions and not a whole lot of answers. But what he did know is that he there for a reason.

When his plane touched down in Flores, Luke was met at the airport by Tomas, his guide, who greeted him at the gate with an infectious smile and a warm handshake.

"Mr. Taylor, It's so nice to meet you. I am Tomas. I will be your guide on the road to El Mirador."

Luke responded with a smile as he fumbled around for his cell phone. "Please call me Luke."

"Yes, well you must be tired and hungry from your trip. Let me show you to your hotel room and then we can see about getting you something to eat."

"That sounds good" Luke agreed as he finally found his cell phone in the front pocket of his backpack. He was anxious to call Stacy, but waited until they were in the car and on the road.

Tomas had parked his car on the curb in front of the airport while he went inside to greet Luke. That's something you could never do in the United States, and the casual laid back vibe of the airport was a false reflection of real life Guatemala. It can be a very dangerous place too.

They got into Tomas's car and pulled away from the curb. The traffic was brisk as they merged into it. Luke finally had a chance to call Stacy, so he turned off the car radio and dialed her up.

"Luke, is that you."

"Yes, it's me."

"How are you? Is everything ok? Where are you?"

He strained to hear her voice because of the horns from a dozen cars that were all trying to be in the same place at the same time. He had to speak up for her to hear him.

"I'm in Guatemala, in a city called Flores. We're leaving in the morning for a village called Santa Maria. It's going to be our base camp."

"Base camp for what?" she asked with a concerned tone.

"We're going up into the high jungle to a place called El Mirador. They said that I was going to meet some kind of ancient Mayan king who is part jaguar or something like that."

Her voice was crackling from a weak connection, but he could still make out what she was saying. Then for no reason the signal improved and her voice was crystal clear.

"This sounds creepy Luke. How long will you be gone?"

"I don't know." he said in a normal tone thanks to the improved reception.

"Well I sure hope you know what you're doing?" Said Stacy

"I do too, Baby. I do too."

"When you get this tattoo it will change you won't it?"

"I don't know. They're talking about superhuman powers. I'm not sure what to expect, but somehow it feels like this is my destiny. Like this is what my whole life has been coming to."

"I know," Stacy said, "I can feel it too. Something's happening."

"They want to tattoo you as well, and they want to do it tomorrow."

"What tattoo?"

"The Mark of K'Na, the patroness of knowledge and wisdom. They said that you would know about things before they happen, and they made it plain that this was something we were both going to do together."

"Should I get the tattoo? What is it they want us to do?"

"Defend the helpless and heal the sick. I don't think there's any more to it than that."

"What do you think I should do Luke?"

"You and I work great together in Miami, and we would be great together here too. But what about the babies, do you think it will hurt the babies?"

"No, I don't think so. I can just feel it in my spirit; we're supposed to do this" she said.

They drove another ten minutes or so until the reception went bad again and she had to raise her voice to be heard.

"You just be careful, Luke."

"Don't worry baby, I have an excellent guide. Hello? Hello?"

"Did you lose her?" asked Tomas.

"Yeah, we got disconnected" Luke said.

"The reception is not so good here sometimes" Tomas said as he pulled the car into the hotel parking lot. He had already checked them in and had the keys, so they took a few minutes to settle their stuff and then made the short walk the Louisa's Cantina.

Louisa's is a festive restaurant, brightly colored in yellow with red and green trim, and draped with strings of bare lightbulbs that provide sufficient light for mingling amidst the drone of conversations and tinkling glasses. Often they will have a guitar player singing Spanish love songs over dinner and the bar serves the best Margarita's in Flores.

They found a table and had dinner. Afterwards, Tomas produced a worn parchment map and went over their plans for the journey.

"We will leave here tomorrow morning and fly to Santa Maria. There we will pick up our supplies and meet our guides. We expect to be gone six or seven days. It's a three day journey each way, and we're bringing enough food for you to stay a couple extra days if you'd like."

"How often have you made this trip?" Luke asked.

"I have never been to El Mirador. Very few people have ever been to EL Mirador. It is the cradle of Mayan civilization, but it was abandoned long ago, and has been reclaimed by the jungle."

"How will you find it? Is it on the map?"

"Yes," Tomas answered, "but it is just a rough guide."

"What do you mean it's just a rough guide?" said Luke.

It was a very old map, on a parchment scroll which he unfurled and spread across the table.

"Where did you get this?" Luke said.

"It was given to me by the Mayan Council of Elders." Tomas replied. "But as you can see, it is just a rough guide. Tikal and Flores are on the map, and we know where they are, so we have those cities as a point of reference. El Mirador appears to be about one hundred and fifty miles northwest of Flores, so we will try to find El Mirador by compass. We know approximately where it is, but very few men have actually been there. My understanding is that one of our guides has been there before."

"Well that's good to know," Luke sighed as he sat back in his seat, daunted by the task that lay ahead, "but it's not very reassuring."

"We will do fine" said Tomas. "We will have experienced jungle guides and plenty of supplies. I think you will find what you are looking for."

"Yes, that's what I'm afraid of" Luke said, only half serious. He was anxious to find out what was waiting for him at El Mirador, and at the same time, he was concerned about the unknown and the rigors of the trip.

He went to bed that night with Stacy's words echoing in his head. El Diablo would strike again, and soon. The only answer was for him to get the Mark of the Feathered Serpent and destroy him once and for all. But that would be easier said than done, and in the meantime, the criminal was free to create havoc.

El Diablo was determined to capture Luke and get the Feathered Serpent tattoo. He knew about Tomas, and had been able to read the man's mind and find out that Luke was to receive the Mark of the Feathered Serpent himself. The criminal knew that once Luke got the tattoo he would be very difficult to stop, and he was determined not to let that happen.

Early the next morning, Tomas banged on Luke's door.

"Luke, are you ready?" he said.

"Almost" Luke answered as he shoved the last of his

stuff into his backpack.

They checked out of the hotel and took a Taxi out to a small private airstrip where they picked up another single propeller airplane.

"No matter how many times he had flown in one of these little planes it never gets any easier" Luke thought to himself as he strapped himself in and checked it twice to be safe. "It's like taking your car out to the airport and driving down the runway at eighty or ninety miles an hour until the car suddenly begins to lift off the ground. I try not to look."

After about an hour in the air they landed on the small airstrip that serves the village of Santa Maria. "This place looks too small for even this small runway" Luke said.

"It's for shipping out the rubber they harvest from the rubber trees that grow here in abundance" Tomas answered.

Later they learned that the airstrip had really been built by looters to ship out ancient Mayan antiquities that were illegally scavenged from the ruins that are in such abundance in the Mirador basin.

They walked to a stable where horses and donkeys were being kept. Tomas spoke with two men who were standing by, and then brought Luke over to meet them.

"Luke, this is Jose and Manuel; they will be our guides to El Mirador."

"It's nice to meet you. Does either of you gentlemen speak English?" Luke asked.

"Si" said Jose.

"Tomas told me you've been to El Mirador."

"Si, three days."

"Yes, it's a three day trip," Tomas added, "each way. And we're bringing enough supplies that you can stay there an extra day or two if you would like."

"When do we start?" Luke asked.

"Now" said Tomas.

He turned and said something to the guides in Spanish, then led Luke to the pin where the animals were being kept. The guides started methodically loading supplies for the trip on horses. There were three of them, carrying food and water, along with the other equipment necessary to survive six or seven days in the jungle.

Tomas took a horse by the reins from one of the stable workers and led it over to Luke.

"When is the last time you were on a horse?" he asked.

"I haven't been on a horse since I was a kid." Luke replied.

"Well, this horse is very gentle. I will stay with you and you will be fine."

"I hope so" Luke said as Tomas helped him into the saddle.

When everyone was mounted, the guides took them out. Jose led the way, followed by Tomas and Luke; than Manuel, who led the horses from the rear. They made their way out of town on a well-traveled trail. It led them into the jungle until every trace of the village was far behind. They rode single file, and after about two hours they stopped for a short break.

"How far will we go today?" Luke asked.

"We will travel ten miles before we stop for the night." Tomas said.

"Why is it that we carry so much water?"

"There is no water here in the jungle. There are only a few rivers or streams. The only water we have is what we bring with us. Without water you won't last very long out here. Men have killed one another over water in the jungle."

Suddenly, and without warning, Jose drew his machete. He reached down and cut the head off a snake that was crawling within inches of Luke's boot. It all happened so fast that Luke was startled at first before he realized what was going on. Tomas just looked at him with a sigh of relief and said "I don't think you want that fellow crawling up your leg."

"No. Thank you." Luke replied.

"Around here you have to walk with one eye on the ground all the time because of these snakes." Tomas said. "They're everywhere. This fellow here is a coral snake, his venom is among the deadliest known to man."

"It must be fatal." Luke said.

"They call this one the twenty minute snake. If he bites you you'll be dead in twenty minutes."

"*I'm a long way from Miami*" Luke thought to himself as they remounted their horses and headed back out on the trail.

The trail led them through an abandoned encampment. Men from the village come out to harvest the rubber trees that grow abundantly here. But from there on the trail broke down dramatically. It had rained the day before, even though the rainy season wasn't due to start for several more weeks; so they dismounted their horses and lead them on foot.

They continued on for two more hours until the guides decided that they should stop for the night. They all pitched in to prepare the campsite and make space for their crude sleeping arrangements.

Jose and Manuel unpacked the animals and secured them. They set up four sleepers, which consisted of hammocks strung between two sturdy trees that are designed to keep you safely off the ground. Then they put up mosquito netting to protect them from the insects that grow to the size of a small bird there in the jungle. They made a fire and passed out caned rations, which represented the safest and most practical way to carry food on a journey like this one.

While they were setting up the camp the horses were restless. At one point Luke thought that they might break free and run off, which was a frightening thought considering the circumstances. But they eventually settled down.

As they ate, Luke noticed that Jose and Manuel were distracted and deep in conversation about something on the ground. Luke ignored them at first, but couldn't help noticing how serious they were. So he walked over to where they were standing to check it out. They spoke in Spanish, while Jose kept pointing at the ground. Finally, Tomas came over to get a look.

"What are they looking at?" he asked.

Jose got down on one knee and showed them.

"They are looking at footprints, Jaguar footprints. They're fairly fresh, and encircle the camp" said Tomas. "The Jaguar is stalking us. The big cats have been known to stalk their prey for days at a time before they strike at a perceived weakness."

Jose said something is Spanish to Manuel, than checked his rifle.

"We will take turns keeping watch" Tomas said. "The horses will let us know if the jaguar comes near the camp. But still, I will sleep better knowing that someone is standing by with a rifle, just in case."

We all agreed, and Luke volunteered to take the first watch. He couldn't have slept if he wanted to. He was exhausted from the day's journey, and yet his adrenaline coursed hot through his veins. Less than two weeks ago he was in Miami, working with Stacy in their tattoo shop. Now, he's deep in the heart of Guatemala, camping in the mountains and traversing the jungle with a rifle in my hands to protect himself from jaguars. *"How the hell did this happen in a matter of ten days of so?"* he asked himself.

After a couple of hours of standing watch, Luke awakened Jose whose job it was to relieve him. He climbed into his hammock, and with a little fidgeting he was able to get settled. As he laid there listening to the sounds of the jungle at night, Luke was sure that he wouldn't get any sleep. But he finally drifted off for a few hours before the morning sun greeted him.

Chapter 21

El Diablo needed money. The constant war with the Prince was expensive and he needed a big score to replace the men and supplies he had lost.

He got word the Columbians had a large shipment of cocaine coming into Honduras in the next few days. It was coming up by boat to San Miguel, a small fishing village on the southwest coast. There's an inlet there; just large enough to dock the boat, and yet small enough to be easily hidden. The cocaine gets transferred into trucks that will carry the drugs through the treacherous mountain roads of Honduras and Guatemala and on to their eventual destination in Mexico. If he could hijack the cocaine, he could sell it himself and get the money he needed to rearm.

El Diablo was sitting in his office, scheming and getting drunk with Jose, his right-hand man. Jose had been a captain at the Prince's security company, but El Diablo corrupted him with money and women. Because he was such a well-known associate of the Prince, the loss was especially hard. In addition, Jose had a lot of inside information about the Prince's organization, and El Diablo was able to exploit it.

He had worked up a plan to steal the cocaine from the Columbians and blame it on the Prince. The Columbians were well acquainted with the Prince, and distrusted him because of his close connections with the Honduran Army. It wouldn't take much to convince them it was the Prince who had robbed them. And the one thing everybody knew about the Columbians was if they thought you had stolen from them, or misled them – your days on this earth would be numbered.

"When will the boat dock?" El Diablo asked.

"I believe it will arrive somewhere between four and six-o'clock. We will know when they leave Columbia, and considering the weather, I am comfortable with the estimate."

"What about the trucks?" El Diablo said as he threw down another shot of tequila.

"Don Garcia has been transporting the Columbian's cocaine for over three years. They have a system and they follow it every time. They normally bring three trucks; one to haul the cocaine, and two others, one in front and one in the rear to defend the drugs." Then he added, "Pour me another shot."

El Diablo gave Jose a look that said, *"Did you really just tell me to pour you a drink?"*

Jose froze. He realized what he had said and began to sweat. He stood up and reached over the table and picked up the bottle. Then he looked up at his boss and said, "Can I pour you another shot?" at which point he sat down.

"How many men are we taking?" El Diablo continued.

"Fourteen. It will be enough. We will arrive by two o'clock and assemble in a clearing that's about six miles from the dock. Once we know Don Garcia's men are in place, our trucks will bring us within a mile of it. We'll walk the last mile through the jungle and come up on them from behind."

"What if they find out about it and you lose the element of surprise?" El Diablo said.

"We'll be in for an old fashion fire fight. But if we can surprise them from behind, we can trap them with their backs to the water and no place to hide. We'll kill them all and drag the bodies into the jungle," Jose said. "When the ship arrives we can commandeer it, steal the drugs, and send them away believing that the Prince is responsible. Even his connections in the Military won't be able to get him out of this one."

Earlier that morning, Stacy met the Prince on the rooftop. He met her at the door, walked her to the chopper, and helped her aboard.

"Good morning," she said as she strained to make the step up into the chopper. Being seven months pregnant makes everything more difficult.

"Are you ready?" he asked her. "This is a big honor."

"I don't know what to expect," Stacy said as she struggled with the seatbelt.

The Prince saw her and reached in to help. There were also four of the Prince's men on the roof, all heavily armed, who boarded the second chopper.

Mike was at the controls this morning. He was busy studying weather patterns on his iPad, and was so engrossed that he didn't even notice Stacy at first. When he finally looked up, he gave her a big smile and a nod and then turned his attention to the Prince."

"We have some rough weather heading our way Boss, but I think we can make it to Copan before the worst of it hits."

"Ok Mike, take us out then" said then Prince. So Mike lifted the big bird up and took her out, over the city and the jungle, until it found its way to the clearing in Copan.

"Why are all these men coming with us?" Stacy whispered in the Prince's ear.

"I promised Luke I would watch out for you, so we're not taking any chances. And if El Diablo knew that you were to receive the Mark of K'Na, he would do whatever he could to prevent that from happening."

"Why?"

"Because he understands how dangerous it is for him if you get this tattoo. You will see events before they happen, and know what is in the hearts and minds of men; both good and evil. It will be very difficult for him to get to you because you will always be one step ahead of him. Luke will depend on you for wisdom and guidance as Kukulcan leads you."

"What about Luke? When I spoke with him last night he said they were looking for a lost city and a Jaguar King. Do you know what he's talking about?"

"He is talking about the lost city of El Mirador. It is the birthplace of the Maya, and it is in the temple of the Jaguar King that Luke will receive the Mark of the Feathered Serpent."

"What does it all mean? I understand that he's going to have extraordinary abilities, but why? What do they want from us?"

"Luke has been selected by Kukulcan to receive the Mark of the Feathered Serpent. The warrior / healer moves and lives among the people, and is the guardian of the weak."

"How will we know what to do?" Stacy asked.

"Kukulcan will lead you. Your life will change. It will never be the same after this."

When they arrived in Copan, the van was waiting to take Stacy, the Prince and his men to the ruins. They waited in the usual place for Dario to meet them.

Dario had been instructed to bring Stacy to the Ceremonial Chamber where she was to receive the tattoo. The Shaman was already there and he was ready for her. Everyone sat down as he raised his hands, closed his eyes, and began to pray in Mayan. Dario also began chanting prayers. They prayed and called upon Kukulcan to make his presence felt.

After several minutes, the room gradually began to feel electric. The hairs on Stacy's arms were standing up, and she could feel her body tingling. Even the babies started moving around. Heaviness fell on the chamber, and the presence of Kukulkan filled the place. Stacy tried to move but was unable to. They all sat in a trance, and Kukulkan spoke to Stacy's spirit.

"Today you will receive the Mark of K'Na, the patroness of wisdom and knowledge. I will open your mind and lead you into understanding. You will have visions and see the future. You will know danger, but will have no fear. You will guide your husband on his journey, and together you will destroy the evil one."

They continued to pray in Mayan, and as they did, the heaviness eventually lifted and the presence of Kukulcan faded.

Everyone sat silently for a few minutes and then the Shaman looked at Stacy and asked her "Do you understand what just happened?"

He spoke in Mayan and Dario translated for her.

"I'm not sure," Stacy said.

"Kukulkan has chosen you. You have been anointed to carry the Mark of K'Na. Your wisdom will guide Luke, and in your spirit you will hear his voice. You will be his hands to destroy El Diablo."

The tattoo makes a ring around the left arm in a geometric shape that resembles ocean waves that are black and outlined in red, and the Shaman would do Stacy's tattoo personally. Dario had already received extensive tattoo training and the Shaman had every confidence that he would do it correctly, but there are certain tattoos that only a Shaman can do, and this was one of them.

Stacy was no stranger to the needle, but this was different. The bone needle and the mallet inflicted a whole new level of pain into the equation. And while she had no doubt that the traditional way was the best way to do these tattoos, she was concerned about the babies, and determined that if she thinks that the trauma is too much for them that she would stop the tattoo wherever they were in the process.

As one of Miami's top tattoo artists, Stacy had been on both sides of the needle many times, and she prided herself in her stoic body language as she was being inked. It was a badge of honor. But this was different.

The Shaman's first tap with the mallet established early that this was going to hurt badly. Stacy showed no emotion as the Shaman continued to tap, tap, tap; forcing the ink under the skin. And just like all the other tattoos, the ink came alive as soon as it touched her.

Stacy already had a tattoo on her arm where the mark of K'Na would go, but as the ink entered her skin the old tattoo began to fade away to make room for the new one. The Shaman continued to tap in the same spot, over and over again, making sure the ink was evenly distributed. And while The Shaman had seen many men wince in pain, Stacy sat in silence. A lone tear that ran down her face was the only sign of her suffering.

When it was over, the Shaman took time to explain to Stacy what would happen and Dario translated.

"How do you feel?"

Stacy gave a weak smile but said nothing.

Dario helped her back to the van that would drive them to the Prince's landing strip. The helicopter had them back in San Pedro Sula and up in the Penthouse in less than an hour.

She drew a hot bath and eased herself in. She had been concerned about the stress of the tattoo ordeal on her pregnancy, but she was fine at each step of the way, and they were able to finish it without incident.

After her bath, she went to bed and rested. Now things would never be the same. Now they were on this journey together.

Chapter 22

The next morning Luke awakened to the sounds of the jungle; a plethora of different animals screaming *good morning* at the top of their lungs. And even though it was only seven o'clock, the temperature was already eighty-five degrees and the humidity was "off the chart."

The group gathered their things together, broke camp and headed back out on the trail. They were determined to push harder that middle day, so they could get to El Mirador earlier on the third day. That's assuming, of course, that Jose actually knows how to find it.

As they traveled down the jungle trail the guides keep an eye on the rain clouds which were starting to organize. The beginning of the rainy season was still several weeks away, but somebody forgot to tell Mother Nature.

There had been heavy rains off and on over the last

couple of days, and it looked like it would rain again today; and with the rain came the mud. In some places the trail broke down to almost nothing. Jose and Tomas dismounted and continued on foot, leading their horses and slicing out a trail through the jungle foliage with their machetes. They traveled hard for several hours, thrashing their way through the jungle before they stopped to rest. After walking and clearing brush for the last two hours, Tomas was exhausted and sat down to rest on a fallen tree. Luke reached for his canteen, took a drink, and walked over to where he was sitting.

"How are we doing?" Luke asked in between swigs of water. He caught Jose and Manuel, out of the corner of his eye, kneeling down to examine the tracks that seemed to follow them. Tomas walked over to check it out for himself.

"More jaguar footprints" he said as he reached for his own canteen, "the big cat is stalking us."

"What should we do?" Luke asked.

Tomas walked back over to where his horse was tied and retrieved his rifle.

"There's nothing we can do" he said "except to be ready and stay vigilant. The horses will let us know if it gets too close. Just make sure you can get to your rifle quickly because these cats move fast."

We rested for about thirty minutes before we remounted and started back out. The road was a little better in some places, and Jose would alternate between riding and walking so he could continue to clear the field.

Giant insects were everywhere, and the rains just seemed to bring them out in droves. Some of them were so large that their fluttering wings could be mistaken for a small bird. Everyone had been instructed to wear white long-sleeve cotton shirts that would make it easier to spot bugs before they have a chance in attach themselves to you.

As they continued to make their way, Luke could begin to smell the rain in the air. It was subtle at first, but began to get stronger by the minute until the raindrops finally began to fall.

The trail was so thin that the only way to ride was single file. Luke hurried up and pulled close enough to Tomas to get his attention.

"What will we do about the rain?" he said.

"There's not much we can do" Tomas replied, "except to try to find cover, although there's not much to be had out here."

"Yeah, I noticed." Luke said.

They continued on for another ten minutes until the rain began to come down so hard that they were forced to stop. The animals were secured to trees, and they found thick foliage that they could use for shelter.

The smell in the air was remarkable; a combination of the pure rain water and the earthy plant life. It rained so hard that at times Luke couldn't see more than a few feet in front of him, and the rhythm of the rain called out the image of jungle drums.

When the rain got stronger, it became more difficult to stay out of it. Within minutes it became so strong that it cut through their makeshift shelter and drenched them. The rain continued for at least another twenty minutes, and as it did, Luke could see that the trail was disintegrating into a muddy mess.

As the rain finally started to let up the horses began to get restless. It was subtle at first, but they quickly began to complain at the top of their lungs and fight against the reins that held them down. In a flash Luke remembered what Tomas had said about keeping his rifle close by. He panicked when he realized that his only weapon was on his horse, so he walked as fast as he could to get it.

There was a rustling in the brush that moved quickly. Luke got a glimpse of it, but it went by so fast that he couldn't make out what it was. He feared that it might be the jaguar.

The rain finally let up enough for them to head back out again, so they did. But this time the trail had been washed out and the ground was so muddy that it was nearly impassable. They slogged away, a few feet at a time, pulling the horses along and trying their best to keep from getting stuck. Each step was an effort, and Luke found himself starting to wonder if they were even going the right way.

They continued for several more hours. The sun came out and scorched the land and eventually dried the mud enough to make movement possible. This time, however, there was no trail at all; so they stopped to get our bearings.

Tomas reached into his saddlebag and produced the map.

"Are we going the right way?" Luke asked as he reached around to feel for his rifle, just in case. It was reassuring to have it by his side.

"Yes, El Mirador is located approximately forty miles north from Santa Maria, where we started" Tomas said. He fished into his pants pocket for a beat up old compass which he laid on the map to determine if we were headed in the right direction.

"If we can find one of the causeways we'll find the city" Tomas said.

"What do you mean causeway?" Luke asked.

"The Mayans built causeways connecting the major cities together here in the Mirador Basin. Most of these limestone highways have been buried over time, but if we can find one of those, we could follow it on into the City.

"That would be too easy" Luke thought to himself. "How much further do we have to go today?"

"The rain has put us behind schedule," said Tomas as he carefully rolled up the map and stuck it back in his saddlebag. "If we hope to reach El Mirador before sundown tomorrow, we will need to cover at least four more miles before we camp for the night."

Jose and Manuel checked on the animals to make sure their gear had survived the rain, and then they took off again. They alternated between riding and walking the horses. The plant life was so thick in places that they had to hack their way through it. Other times they were able to ride. But always, Luke had the sensation of being watched. And they all knew to be alert in case they were still being stalked.

After several more hours they decided to make camp for the night. They worked together to clear a space and secure the animals. They strung their hammocks with the mosquito netting, and Manuel put together the kitchen and started dinner.

Luke walked the perimeter of the camp with Tomas and Jose looking for jaguar footprints. The big cat was definitely following them, and he was getting closer and closer to the camp. Tomas and Jose insisted that we take turns standing watch for the jaguar, and everyone kept their rifles close by at all times.

After dinner, they sat around the fire and Luke listened as Tomas told stories about ancient Mayan kings, and wars between rival cities.

"Although nobody actually knows why," he said "it is believed that the residents of El Mirador fled the city and went north to create a new city, Calakmul. It was the archrival of Tikal, the largest and most powerful city in the Mayan universe."

"Calakmul forged alliances with smaller cities to surround and control Tikal. So, in the year 670 ad, Nun Bak Chak, the King of Tikal launched a two-pronged attack on the cities, hoping to gain control of territory to the west, and to disrupt Calakmul's lucrative trade route to the southern highlands.

"Yuknoom the Great, the King of Calakmul, engaged and defeated Tikal. He captured their King, Nun Bak Chak, and brought him back to Calakmul to be paraded in the streets. The King was tortured, and then sacrificed to Kukulcan, the god of war."

"Tikal had raised an army that was far superior in numbers to the warriors of Calakmul. But many of the warriors of Calakmul wore the Mark of the Feathered Serpent, tattooed on the inside of each warriors forearm. They had the speed and strength of the jungle cats, and were virtually unbeatable in battle."

"Where did they get the tattoos?" Luke asked as he kept on one eye on the brush watching for the Jaguar, and the other eye on the ground watching for snakes.

"The Temple of the Jaguar at El Mirador. The spirit of the Jaguar King guards the temple and protects it from looters."

"How will he know who we are?"

"Kukulcan will guide him and he will know."

"What about this, I already have a tattoo in that spot?" Luke said as he rolled up his shirt sleeve to reveal a very detailed and colorful tattoo that covered his arm from his shoulder to his wrist.

"Don't worry," Tomas said as he stood up and began getting ready for bed, "the Spirit of the King will know." And with that Luke retired as well. He would take the second shift guarding the camp, so he wanted to get as much sleep before that as he could.

Tomorrow he hoped to find El Mirador.

El Diablo arrived at his office around nine o'clock the next morning. His men had assembled and were waiting for him. He was particularly intense, and no one dared speak to him unless he spoke first.

He surrounded himself with thugs. These were very bad men who killed without a second thought. And because he paid them so well, he was able to recruit some of the most dangerous men in Honduras.

He changed his location every week to make it almost impossible to find him. That day, he was working out of an abandoned storage facility. As he entered the room, Jose met him at the door.

"Good morning, Boss."

El Diablo turned his eyes slightly to acknowledge he at least heard Jose.

He walked into the makeshift office with Jose trailing behind. It was a complete trash heap, but somehow El Diablo looked like he belonged there. He reached into his pocket and pulled out a cigar. He bit the end off and lit it with a stick match. Someone brought him a cup of coffee, and he sat back in his chair to review the preparations for the raid at San Miguel.

"When did the boat leave?"

"It left at seven-thirty, so it should dock in San Miguel around four-thirty; right on schedule," Jose said.

"Do we know how many men they have on board?"

"Our man in Columbia thinks there are at least fifteen armed guards, plus a three-man crew. We'll leave here at ten-o'clock. It's a two-hour flight to Tegucigalpa where the trucks will be waiting to take us to San Miguel. It will be another two-hour drive to the staging area. That will get us there with at least an hour to spare."

"Ok. I have four more men coming shortly who will join us on the raid. Once they get here we can leave."

"Who are these men?" Jose said.

"I don't know, and I don't care. My men pulled these guys off the street yesterday, and the Shaman gave them the Mark of the Feathered Serpent."

"What about the Curse?"

"They're almost there. They have all nearly lost their minds, and are beginning to become agitated. They will be fearless soon because they have no fear of death. And in the end, if they survive the raid they will kill themselves."

Jose was on his way to get El Diablo another cup of

coffee when he spotted them walking in the door. There were four of them, each more evil looking than the next, with the look of death in their eyes. Their instructions were to report to El Diablo

He called Jose over and instructed the four men to do whatever Jose said. He had used his mind control to get into their heads and make them commit murder.

"I will stay in the Jungle while you lead the raid," said El Diablo.

"You can't afford to have anyone see your face," Jose agreed

"Some people would recognize me, and the Columbians would know I was the one who stole their cocaine."

"Some of them will recognize me too, but they think I still work for the Prince."

"Yes, and that's just what we want them to think. Maybe they will kill the Prince and save me the trouble."

El Diablo stood up and walked to the truck that would transport him and his men to the landing strip. Everyone followed. It was a seven-mile drive to the airstrip where the planes were waiting for them.

When they finally arrived, they boarded the planes and prepared for take-off. Soon they were airborne. The two-hour flight would take them to Tegucigalpa, the capital city of Honduras. It's a modern city of nearly two million people, with opulent walled estates surrounded by heartbreaking slums. And like San Pedro Sula, it's one of the most dangerous cities in the world.

The three planes that carried El Diablo and his thugs found their way to a tiny, secluded landing strip. They taxied to the end of the runway where three trucks were waiting to take them out to the staging area.

After a two-hour drive, they arrived at their destination and waited. The Garcia group had been transporting the Columbian's cocaine for over three years and ran a very professional operation. El Diablo was confident they would arrive on time, and positioned a man in the jungle near the dock to give the signal when the trucks got there.

They waited about an hour before the boat arrived. El Diablo got the signal, so he and his men jumped into their trucks and drove the five miles from the staging area to the drop off point. The truck drivers were instructed to turn the trucks around and prepare for a fast getaway if things went bad.

El Diablo had twenty men all together, counting Jose and himself. He led them through the jungle until they reached the dock. He had Garcia's crew right where he wanted them. His thugs were less than two hundred feet from the dock, and the Garcia men were trapped with their backs to the water.

He hesitated for a moment to give everyone a chance to lock in on a target, and then he gave the order to kill.

El Diablo's thugs opened up on Garcia's men from behind trees. The killing went quickly because there was no place for Garcia's men to hide. Three of his men jumped into the water and tried to swim away, but EL Diablo's homicidal maniacs followed and swam so fast they were able to catch Garcia's men in a matter of seconds. They beat them without mercy, and held their heads under the water until they were dead. Then they swam back to the dock where El Diablo's thugs had finished off Garcia's men and were dragging their dead bodies into the jungle and out of sight before the Columbians arrived.

El Diablo stepped out of the jungle to inspect the carnage. As he waded through the bodies of Garcia's men, he periodically found one that was still alive. When he did, he put his rifle to the man's head and shot him point blank, spilling his brains all over the ground.

After the area was cleared, El Diablo's men waited for the shipment to come in. He had lost three men in the firefight, but was confident he would prevail over the Columbians. He had four homicidal maniacs that carried the counterfeit Mark of the Feathered Serpent. And even though they would be dead before the day is over, they were a powerful tool in El Diablo's hands to crush the Prince and control Luke once and for all. He was determined to get his revenge, and he was determined to get the Mark of the Feathered Serpent.

At four-thirty the ship arrived right on schedule. El Diablo had the four men who had received the counterfeit tattoos, plus Jose, waiting on the shore to greet the Columbians. He had another six men hidden in one of the trucks, and three more in the jungle with El Diablo.

When the boat reached its destination, two of the crew members jumped onto the dock to secure the vessel. They tied her down, and walked down the dock towards Jose. As they approached him, El Diablo reached into their minds from the jungle where he was hiding. He was able to make the Columbians think that Jose was a good friend, and they greeted him warmly. EL Diablo had given strict instructions that the crew was to be spared, and Jose knew he would be held responsible if anything happened, so he handled the crew himself.

The four homicidal maniacs boarded the ship before the ship's Captain or the guards realized what was happening, and once they did, it was too late. The killers waited until they were onboard to begin the killing. They split up and opened fire at close range, killing the Columbians in cold blood.

The fight only lasted about five minutes, and when it was over, two of the killers and nearly all of the Columbians lay dead on the boat. The other two killers walked among the bodies, looking for survivors. They found several who were badly wounded, but still alive, and finished them off.

El Diablo had instructed his men to spare the ship's crew and two of the Columbians. He wanted to send them home with a message. So Jose forced one of the two guards, whose hands were already bound, to his knees. He grabbed him by the hair, drew out his machete, and started hacking off the prisoner's head. It took several hacks to get it off, and the blood ran everywhere. When they had it off, Jose put it in a box and handed it to the other survivor and said "Give this to your boss. Tell him it's a message from the Prince. Your drugs are killing our people. You are a scourge on the land. Leave Honduras. Don't come back. If you do, the same fate awaits you."

El Diablo's men unloaded the cocaine from the boat and put it into the truck. When it had all been unloaded, they let the crew and the survivor board the ship and sail for home.

Now El Diablo had the money to rearm and things were going to get ugly real fast. Once the Columbians found out what happened at San Miguel, they would be back to make an example out of the Prince.

Later that evening, El Diablo sat in his office in silence as he concentrated on Captain Russo, head of Detectives at the San Pedro Sula police force. He placed the thought in the Captains head that the Prince was responsible for the raid at La Cantina and the deaths of four of El Diablo's men. The Captain found several street tuffs who claimed to be eye witnesses and were willing to testify against the Prince. So despite the lack of any real evidence, the Captain issued an arrest warrant for the Prince, charging him with four counts of first degree murder; a charge which carried the death sentence.

Chapter 24

The next morning Luke was up with the sun. He had barely slept the night before, and he was both excited and frightened about what lay ahead.

Miguel was up early and started making breakfast on a flat piece of aluminum that he used for a griddle. Tomas and Jose weren't long after, and made the rounds looking for footprints the jaguar would have made.

Luke secured his things while Miguel distracted everyone with the smell of food being cooked over an open fire. The coffee was made the traditional way. He boiled ground coffee and sugar in a small pan that he placed directly on the griddle. When the coffee is done the grounds sink to the bottom and you can pour it into a cup.

Miguel had brought canned meat, which he cooked directly on the griddle, along with tortillas that he made with corn meal and water. It was truly unlike any breakfast Luke had ever experienced.

After breakfast they saddled their horses, loaded their gear and headed back out onto the trail. At this point they were basically making their own trail, cutting and hacking as they went along. The foliage that grows in some parts of the jungle is relatively sparse, and it can be traversed on horseback. Unfortunately, some of it is so thick that they could barely get through it, even with their combined efforts. It was rigorous work, and after two hours they stopped to rest.

Tomas tied his horse up, and started to sit down to rest. Suddenly a shot rang out. It caught Luke totally by surprise, and it took him several seconds to recover from the shock of the being shot at. He visually did a scan of the clearing they were resting in, and when he did, he saw Tomas on the ground with a rifle wound in his chest.

Luke instinctively ran over to Tomas and fell to his knees beside him. Before he had a chance to react, six men stepped out of the brush; each with a rifle pointed at them. The wound was bad, and he was writhing in pain.

Two of the men walked over to where the horses were tied. They untied them and led them off with all of their food, water and supplies. Then they lined Luke and the guides with their hands behind their heads, and he feared what was coming next – executions.

He glanced at Tomas, who was lying on the ground bleeding profusely, and he could sense that his friend needed help fast.

"Why are you doing this? What do you want?" Luke asked with a good measure of fear in his voice.

"Looters." Jose said to Luke under his breath as the men became distracted and started going through their stuff. "They steal treasures from Mayan temples and gravesites. The pieces they steal are worth a fortune on the black market. But they don't want any witnesses."

Suddenly, without warning, a jaguar leapt from behind a thick layer of brush. It happened so fast that nobody had time to react. The cat leaped upon one of the men and used his sharp claws to rip the man's face open, hitting his juggler vain in the process. The man fell to the ground while trying to stop the bleeding, but to no avail.

Almost immediately, the big cat turned on the other man who had been taking away the horses with their supplies. The man tried to run away but only made it a few steps before the jaguar caught him and literally ripped one of his arms off, causing him to fall on the ground, screaming out in pain and in shock, bleeding at such a rapid rate that he would be dead in a matter of minutes.

The other four looters immediately turned their guns on the Jaguar, but he moved so fast that nobody could get a clean shot at him. The big cat came around behind them and leaped out from behind the trees. He grabbed a third man by the head and dragged him into the bushes, where his blood curdling cries for help could be heard. The other three men disappeared back into the jungle from where they came. The jaguar pursued them, and by the screaming that could be heard, Luke assumed that he had caught up with them.

"Get your rifle" Jose said. He and Manuel did the same and scanned the area for any sign of the jaguar. The looters screams had died down, and the jungle was too quiet for comfort. Even the howler monkeys stopped calling out as the three of them scanned the gruesome scene that was laid out before them.

Jose and Miguel were silent as they wondered into the bush to gather the horses that had scattered at the sound of gunfire. Without the water they carried we would dead in the jungle in only matter of a day or two.

Luke knelt over Tomas and tried to help him. He had some medical training, but he wasn't prepared for something like this.

Tomas was dying, and if he didn't do something fast it would be too late. So Luke closed his eyes and began to chant Mayan prayers until Kukulcan made his presence felt. He spoke to Luke's spirit, although no audible sound could be heard, and led him into understanding. He was to give Tomas the butterfly of life.

Fortunately, they returned the horses quickly and Luke's tattoo kit was in still in his saddlebags. Luke ran over to where his horse was secured and retrieved his tools. He turned around and quickly ran back to Tomas and fell to his knees beside him. He pulled the correct needle from the satchel, as Kukulcan guided his hand, and began tapping the ink into Tomas's arm. As soon as he did you could see an immediate improvement in his condition. And as Luke continued to do the tattoo, Tomas continued to improve by the minute.

It took over an hour to complete the tattoo, but when it was finished, Tomas was totally healed, and there was no sign of the bullet wound.

The events of the last two hours had them all shaken, but they feared that the jaguar would return, so they collected their things and headed back out and onto the trail.

They fought their way through the jungle foliage for another couple of hours when Jose suddenly stopped his horse and dismounted. He called Manuel over and they both kept looking and touching the ground. Tomas called out "what is it?"

"I think we found the causeway," Jose said as he reached into the bag of tools loaded onto one of the horses.

"How do you know?" Luke asked.

"Here, look here." Jose said as he pointed to a spot on the trail where a small piece of limestone could be seen.

The ancient highway was uncovered by heavy rains, and fortunately Jose spotted it.

He produced a shovel and walked back over to where he had been standing. By this time we had all secured our horses, and were standing in a circle watching Jose with great interest as he put shovel to dirt. It didn't take more than a minute or so before he found what he was looking for - a piece of a limestone road.

Jose was overjoyed and began clearing the road, turning over dirt and exposing the limestone causeway. They followed the trail, exposing pieces of it as they went to ensure that they were still on track.

They were all very careful to keep their rifles handy out of fear. They all feared that the jaguar would return. Of course, rifles didn't do anything to save the looters, so they weren't overly confident. But there was nothing else they could do except keep moving and hope to fine El Mirador.

After another couple of hours of fighting the jungle they came to what they thought was going to be a clearing, but when they rounded the corner, there it was - El

Mirador.

The Temple of the Jaguar rose above the treetops and dominated the landscape. Luke's senses were attuned to the spirits of a thousand Mayan warriors who have stood in this exact spot at the foot of the Jaguar Temple to receive The Mark of the Feathered Serpent. And as he stared at the temple, his mind focused on his encounter with the jaguar, and he could see why the Mayans held them in such high regard.

Jose kept saying over and over "El Mirador, El Mirador."

"This must be it." Luke said as he dug for his camera.

Tomas was flabbergasted. "I have heard of El Mirador my whole life, but never thought I would see it. What are we supposed to do now?"

Jose began securing the horses and unloading supplies. He called out to Tomas "It's getting dark, and if we don't secure the horses and get our camp set up we'll be in trouble once the sun goes down."

Luke and Tomas jumped in and secured all the sleepers, being careful to get the mosquito netting right. Miguel set up the kitchen and cooked the same thing he has cooked every night since they'd been in the jungle, and Jose lit a fire and a series of torches to lite the campsite after dark.

As they ate dinner, Tomas told them the story of the Jaguar King.

"Stories are still told among the K'iche' Maya about Night Sun, the Jaguar god of terrestrial fire. The stories go back for thousands of years. It has been passed down from generation to generation by our grandfathers of old."

"Who is the Jaguar King?" Luke asked while he kept one eye on the ground looking for snakes.

"Kukulcan found the King when he was a child. His parents had been killed in the jungle, and Kukulcan gave the boy to the Jaguars to raise. They nursed and fed the child, and cared for him like he was one of their own. And as he grew, he developed into a man with the speed and the strength of the Jaguars. His name was Great Fiery Jaguar Paw. He became immortal, and his spirit still guards the temple here at El Mirador. It's the holy temple of the Jaguar King."

After dinner was over, Manuel made a batch of Yagi tea. He informed them that it would be a particularly strong batch, and that it will help them "find what we're looking for." As he passed the tea, Luke filled his cup to the brim and waited impatiently for it to get cool enough to drink.

When it finally cooled enough to sip he began to force it down. He drank it as fast as he could, even though it was burning his mouth. He was impatient and he was determined to find out what was waiting for him, but he wouldn't have to wait long.

His reaction to the tea had been very similar to the first two times he drank it. He immediately became sick and threw-up. Soon after his head began to buzz loudly, and colored lights flashed all around him.

He raised his hands to the heavens and began to chant Mayan prayers. As he did, Tomas and their two guides did the same. The group picked up the intensity as they prayed, and called upon the Jaguar King to show himself. Luke had no idea what he was doing, but he instinctively fell into the pattern of prayer that he had learned in the ceremonial chamber at the Temple of Kukulcan in Copan.

After several minutes of urgent prayer, a ball of terrestrial fire appeared in front of the temple, preventing anyone from getting too close. The powerful presence of Great Fiery Jaguar Paw, the man who became a god, could clearly be felt; and no one dared to speak or move.

Suddenly the unexpected happened. A Jaguar wandered into the campsite before anyone knew he was there. Everyone froze. He was close, and there would be no escape. Luke panicked and did a mental search for his rifle before he remembered that it was by the hammock with the rest of his stuff. Too far to get to if the Jaguar was to strike.

A cold chill shot straight down his spine as the big cat moved through the campsite, weaving in and out of their circle, so close that Luke could feel his hot breath. "

"How could my life end like this?" Luke thought. "What about Stacy? Surely it will just be a matter of seconds before he strikes."

But he didn't.

The big cat turned around and walked right into the fire ball that had been burning brightly the whole time. However, instead of being burned alive, he transformed into the figure of a man and re-emerged from the flames without as much as a headache.

Luke could hardly believe his eyes. The Jaguar King transformed into a man right here before him. He walked his way and stopped within ten feet of him. He spoke to Luke in perfect English.

"You have been chosen Luke. Kukulcan has seen your future. You will be a tool in his hands as he strengthens you

to protect the innocent."

Luke had questions, but he couldn't speak. Yet somehow the Jaguar King read his mind and answered questions that Luke hadn't even asked yet.

"Yes, that was me in the jungle. I have been following you for several days."

"Yes, it was me who killed the looters. I am the guardian of the temple."

"You were chosen because Kukulcan has seen your strength. You don't yet understand your power, but soon you will. And then you will know what you should do. But once you take The Mark of the Feathered Serpent, you can never go back to your old life."

"Somehow I feel like this is my destiny." Luke said.

"That it is, Luke. Hold out your arm." He said

Luke wasn't sure if he would be able to move his arm, but somehow he did, and raised his right arm up for him.

He turned it over palm up and held Luke by the wrist. His other hand had fingers like tattoo needles, and he began using his nails to do the tattoo.

The colors were unbelievable, and as the ink hit his skin, the sleeve he had on his right arm receded to make room for the Mark of the Feathered Serpent. Luke didn't understand it, but it only took a few minutes. It's almost like the tattoo just flowed from his hand and into Luke's arm. And when he was finished, Luke could definitely feel something physical was happening to his body.

"Your strength will grow as you learn how to use the tattoo, and you will not be alone. Your wife has been

empowered with wisdom and knowledge. Listen to her."

Luke sat speechless in front of him, completely mesmerized by the moment, and still barely able to move. Then the Jaguar King stepped back and caused fire to shoot from his hands. It caused a small piece of rock to break away from the temple, then walked over to where Luke was standing and gave it to him

"This sacred stone you hold will save your life. Never let it out of your sight. You will need it to face El Diablo. And when the time comes that you need it, you will know what to do with it."

He said other things that Luke didn't understand right away, but came to him later. And after he was finished, the Jaguar King turned around and walked back into the fire which faded and disappeared.

When it was over, They all four looked at each other in disbelief.

"Did that really happen?" Tomas said. Then he and the other two got a look at Luke's tattoo. "Oh my, look at that tattoo" he said, as they all gathered around for a better look. It's the most beautiful tattoo I've ever seen. How do you feel?"

"Energized." Luke replied. "I feel energized and my body feels alive."

He glanced around the campsite, and the first thing he noticed was his new sharper vision. It was crisp and clear. He could even see in the dark. His hearing was enhanced as well. He could hear a twig snap at a thousand yards.

The next thing Luke noticed was his body strength. He felt like he could run all the way back to Flores. He began to run back and forth, and then around the Temple, at an incredible pace without even being short of breath.

He started up the Temple steps. There are ninety one steps to the top of the Temple at El Mirador, and he ran to the top and back down again at full speed without even breaking a sweat.

"This is unbelievable" Tomas said. "I've never seen anything like it.

As he was still speaking Luke dropped to the ground and started doing pushups. He did ten, twenty, fifty pushups. It felt like he could go on forever. Jose even sat on his back while I was doing the pushups, but it made no difference.

Finally, they sat back and assessed the situation.

"Your running is unbelievable. I've never seen anyone run the stairs at any of the temples like I just saw you do. You're not even winded." Tomas observed.

"I know. This is amazing. We need to get back to Flores; in fact, I need to get back to Honduras. Stacy's in danger as long as El Diablo walks the street, but we'll have to wait until the morning to leave."

They sat and talked for several more hours.

"It's an incredible feeling. My body feels like superman" Luke said before he noticed that he had cut the back of his leg on the stone steps when he was running them.

Tomas examined the wound and determined that the cut was nothing serious. "But you are still venerable to injury. A knife, a gun, and even a rock could bring you down."

"Yes" Luke agreed.

They sat around the fire and talked about what had happened for at least another hour. It had been a life changing experience for all four of them. However, the day's events eventually caught up with them, and they retired to their hammocks exhausted.

Chapter 25

Luke got very little sleep during the night. His blood was racing with thoughts about his new abilities and how to use them. By morning he had come to two undeniable facts: He had been selected for a reason and he would have to face El Diablo.

Manuel made breakfast as the rest of the group broke camp and packed the equipment. They ate and laughed. Spirits were high. They had made an impossible journey and found the lost city of El Mirador. It was a heady experience. They were among the very few living souls that had been there, and now they would head for home, empowered to face El Diablo.

The weather was cooperating that day and they had blue skies and sunshine. They were able to retrace their path and go out the same way they came in. Because of that, the going was much easier, and they were able to cover over twenty miles that first day.

As they set up camp, they all agreed that they'd get back out on the trail at first light. They hoped that they could have another good day like the one they had today. If so, they could make it back to our base camp at Santa Maria before darkness tomorrow.

After dinner, they talked and shared stories for a while, but they were all exhausted and soon were asleep.

The next morning they were all awake and ready to go early. They were determined to get home that day, and Luke had his heart set on a hot shower later on that night. They ate a quick breakfast, finished packing their gear, and headed out. Luke had to control the impulse to run. It was hard to be patient when he was probably capable of running the rest of the way home. He considered the fact that he could probably outrun the horses, but he couldn't leave the others behind, so he bided his time.

After about three hours they stopped to take a break. Luke could have gone on, but he waited for the others. As they rested, Luke noticed the horses acting skittish. He scanned the area for any signs of trouble, but everything was calm. Still, the horses concerned him.

Tomas and Luke made small talk as they rested, but Luke was distracted by the feeling that something was amiss. Tomas saw the concern on Luke's face and asked him about it.

"Luke, what's wrong?"

"I don't know what it is, but there's something that's not right."

The horses continued to be restless, so Luke stood up

and made a walk around the perimeter of our rest area. His eyes scanned the tree line, but he could see nothing out of place. His hearing was razor sharp, and he could hear a symphony of animal life singing the song of the jungle; but there was nothing unusual. Then he caught a smell. It was smoke.

"I smell smoke," Luke said.

"I don't smell anything" Tomas responded. "But it's not unusual to have large areas of the jungle set ablaze. It's the ranchers. They purposely set fire to the jungle to clear out the trees for farm land."

"Si," said Jose. "They are destroying ancient ruins, like El Mirador, that are everywhere out here."

"We should get going" Luke said. So they remounted their horses and headed back out onto the trail. They were able to make good time because the trail that they had forged on the way to El Mirador was still clear enough for them to use. But instead of getting away from the fire they seemed to get closer.

After about twenty minutes they began to encounter smoke. It hung in the air with the smell of wood burning. Luke tried to determine the direction of the fire was and where it was going, but it was hard to tell, even with his enhanced senses.

They continued to follow their trail and were moving at a good clip, but the smoke only seemed to get worse. At one point it was so bad that they were having trouble breathing, and it became obvious that they were moving towards the fire and not away from it.

They all had to cover their nose and mouth to breath and talk through the heavy smoke that hung thick in the air.

Tomas pulled out the map to see if there was another way to Santa Maria.

They could try to go around the fire, but since they had no way of knowing which way it was going, they were risking getting trapped and burned alive. But they couldn't go out the way we came in.

Jose and Manuel knew this jungle better than anyone, and they felt that if we could make it to the river, we could follow it downstream to safety. So we took their advice and headed west towards the river.

The way there was difficult. Through much of it, there was no trail at all, and we had to hack our way through the jungle with the hope of finding the river before the fire finds us.

At one point the fire was so close that Luke could hear the crackle of trees and brush burning. The heat was oppressive, and gave them an ominous sign that fire was near. The horses became so frightened by the fire that was rapidly closing in on them that they could no longer control them and they ran away with all the food and water.

Luke could see the fear in everyone's eyes as the fire got closer, but when we crossed over the next ridge, there it was, the San Pedro River. They all ran as fast as they could and fell exhausted on the river bank with the fire destroying the jungle and everything in it.

Unfortunately, they were only halfway home. They still had to get down river, and they had to do it before dark because they had no supplies.

Back at the Prince's penthouse, Stacy was having breakfast with Mary and Jack. She had been thinking about Luke all morning. She was starting to become more sensitive to her Mark of Knowledge, and couldn't shake the feeling that Luke was in trouble.

"There's something wrong, I just know it" Stacy said. "I was hoping to hear from him today or tomorrow, but somethings wrong. I can feel it."

Just then the Prince arrived for breakfast.

"I can't shake the feeling that something is wrong with Luke" she said.

"What is it?" he asked.

"I don't know exactly what it is, but there's a fire."

The Prince knew enough about The Mark of Knowledge to know that if Stacy is seeing something they should listen. So everyone followed him into his office.

On the wall there was a giant map of Central America. He pointed to a spot on the map.

"This is Santa Maria. They use this as a launching point for exploring the jungle" he said. He drew a forty mile radius around the city.

"They have probably been in this area for the last couple of days" he said.

"My God man, there's nothing but jungle there." Jack said.

"I know" the Prince said as he sat down at his computer and started pulling up weather conditions.

Stacy stood close enough that she could look over his shoulder and see that there were wild fires burning all over the area.

"They're on the river" she said. "I can feel it."

"Oh my God" Jack said. "Are they trapped in there?"

"It looks like it" said the Prince. "They probably made their way to the river to get away from the fire and now they're stuck. Unless they get their hands on a boat they'll be trapped, and there's no good way out. The area is a breeding ground for every kind of alligator and snake known to man. If that's where they are than they won't survive for long in there. And if they try to cross over the river to the other side they will have to face flesh eating fish."

"What can we do?" Stacy said with tears beginning to well up in her eyes.

"I'm going after them, that's what I'm going to do" he said.

He picked up the phone and called the hanger where his company's airplanes and helicopters are housed. The phone rang several times before someone answered.

"Good morning, Golden Shield Security."

"Good morning, this is Juan" (he never refers to himself as *the Prince*).

"Good morning boss."

"Is Mike in the hanger?"

"Sure Mr. Rodriguez, let me get him."

There was a brief pause as they called Mike to the phone.

"Good morning Boss."

"Good morning Mike, I going to need you this morning. How soon can you get a plane ready?"

"They just serviced no.2 and I could have it ready to go whenever you get here."

"Ok, I'll be there in thirty minutes; I'll see you then" the Prince said and hung up the phone.

"What's the plan?" Jack said.

"We're going to fly to Flores, and then take a chopper to this spot here" he said as he pointed at a map. "We will start there and fly up and down the river until we find them. If they got to the river, they will probably be somewhere in this area."

"Count me in" said Jack.

"Ok, that's good. I'll need an extra set of eyes."

"Good" said Jack as he kissed Mary and went back to their room to change. He met the Prince on the roof, and they took a chopper out to a small private airfield where his hanger was located. When they arrived Mike had the plane warmed up and ready to go.

"Good morning Boss."

"Good morning Mike."

"So, where are we going this morning?"

"We are going to pull a couple of friends out of a little jam."

Mike laid maps and charts out on a table and they spent several minutes going over the route until they were comfortable. Weather conditions were good for flying but they were also good for fires. It would be over a hundred degrees with no rain in sight; and smoke was going to be a factor.

Once they were set, Mike loaded them all up and taxied out to the runway.

"Beautiful day for flying, is it not?"

"Yes it is Mike. Yes it is." Replied the Prince.

The plane lifted off as it sped down the runway. The Prince leaned into Jack and whispered "That's why I love flying with Mike. He can be somewhat of a cowboy, but the man simply loves to fly. It doesn't matter if it's the plane or the helicopter; he's a hell of a pilot."

Back at the river, Luke was prepared to swim across it, but Jose and Manuel convinced him that if he did, the fish would make him regret it. But they couldn't stay where they were because the fire was burning closer.

"We can't stay here" Luke said as he started walking up river. "We'll get burned alive. We'll have to try to stay ahead of the fire."

"And we have to stay ahead of the coral snakes" said Tomas as he pulled his machete and pointed it at a snake that was making his way out of the jungle and onto the shore. "They'll come out in droves to escape the fire."

Luke wanted to run for safety, but he couldn't leave the others behind, so they all moved at a quick pace. They were able to stay ahead of the fire, but after three hours the others were tired so they stopped to rest.

After a two hour flight Mike landed the group in Flores. There was already a helicopter waiting for them. They made a brief stop to get some equipment and supplies, and then climbed aboard and headed out.

Mike flew the group over the jungle until they reached a predetermined spot. The Prince reviewed the chart and directed Mike down river.

"If they're on the river, they probably haven't gotten this far."

"I agree" Mike said as he swung around and started down the river.

They flew for about twenty minutes, with all eyes looking on both sides of the river. But it was becoming more difficult to see because of the smoke that was getting heaver by the minute.

"If we're going to find them I'm going to have to fly lower." The pilot warned.

"How low can you take it Mike?"

"I can bring her down to within about fifty feet over the water, but it's dangerous. If we get caught up in the trees we're all going to be dead before the days over."

"Do what you've got to do, Mike."

"I thought you'd never ask" he said with a grin, then took them down right over the river.

Tomas stood up after a few minutes and motioned for the exhausted group to get back up. Luke was glad, and couldn't get going fast enough; but he had to slow down so they could keep up.

They walked at a rapid pace, but Luke suspected that it wasn't going to be fast enough. The smoke was getting stronger, and it was evident that we were not going to outrun the fire. He weighed the options, and none of the options were very good; but right at that moment, he heard a sound.

"Wait." he said. "Do you hear that?"

"No" said Tomas. "What do you hear?"

"It's a humming sound" Luke said, but Jose and Manuel didn't hear it either.

"No, wait." Luke insisted, "Listen."

Everyone stood in silence, struggling to hear what

Luke was hearing. Then after a few minutes they all heard it.

There it was. It was getting louder. Everyone held their breath in silent anticipation as Luke listened. Then a big smile came over his face.

"What is it, what is it" said Tomas.

"It's a helicopter" Luke said. "It's a helicopter."

Everyone exploded in laughter and applause.

"Who do you think it is?" Tomas asked.

"If I were a betting man, I'd bet it's the Prince" Luke replied. And as they stood there listening, the humming got gradually louder until the chopper was right upon them.

Mike tugged at the Prince's shoulder and pointed down. "There they are." He said.

Jack spotted them at the same time.

"We'll lower down a cable and pull them up" the Prince said as he moved around to the back of the chopper and grabbed the harness. He had brought along another man to help with the extraction, but Jack wasn't having any of it. He grabbed the harness from the Prince and started to hook himself up.

"How do you hook this together?"

"Here, let me help you" said the Prince as he strapped Jack into the harness. "We're going to lower you down. When you reach the bottom, unstrap the harness and hook the others up. We'll pull them up one at a time."

The Prince controlled the cable, and as soon as Jack was strapped in he began to lower him down. Even though it was only fifty feet it seemed to take forever, but eventually Jack reached the ground.

"Luke, are you alright?" Jack said.

"I thought you'd never get here" He replied with a huge smile.

"Well let's get you guys out of here" Jack said as he unhooked the harness.

As soon as he did he put the harness on Jose who was more than a little apprehensive about the whole thing, and strapped him in. Once he was secure, the Prince began raising Jose up while Mike was fighting to keep the chopper out of the trees.

Once Jose was up they repeated the process until everyone was safely on board. Luke and the others looked really bad, but there were no serious injuries.

The Prince looked at the four of them and laughed out loud. "You fellows could really use a bath." He teased.

"Nice one Juan" Luke replied. "We've been lost in a remote jungle and nearly burned alive by wild fire and that's all you can say?"

Everyone laughed and gave a big sigh of relief as Mike carried them over the jungle and towards home.

Chapter 26

The next morning, the whole group had breakfast together.

Jack and Mary had stayed in the Penthouse with Max yesterday, addressing various issues that had arisen since they left Miami. His foundation was having its annual fund-raising gala, and this was the first year that Jack, Mary, or Max would miss it.

Rosa and Stacy's Uncle spent their time studying and cataloging the Prince's collection of Mayan art and relics. It was better than many museum pieces that they had seen, and Uncle Robert was hoping to find a clue as to why the Mayans just abandoned their cities.

The Prince was still working the streets. He had as many of his men as he could working hard on it, but so far all they could come up with was two locations El Diablo and his thugs had previously used, but had long since abandoned. Colonel Morales had ordered daily aerial sweeps of the jungle, hoping to find El Diablo's location, but they had no luck.

Stacy had gone through her tattoo ordeal, and she was already beginning to develop a sixth sense. At breakfast she knew what people were going to say or do before they did it.

"Luke, there's something happening to me."

"I know. I can sense it."

"Watch, Mary is going to ask the waiter for more coffee." And she did. Then Stacy predicted that Max would excuse himself and go to the restroom, and he did.

"It's the tattoo" Luke said. "It's working on you faster than I expected. Can you control it?"

"I'm not sure, but I think so. It only works when I'm thinking about it."

She also predicted that the Prince's phone would ring, and it did. She even knew who it was.

I noticed the look on the Prince's face as he listened to what was being said on the other end of the phone and he looked concerned.

"What's the matter?" Luke asked.

"It's the police," said Stacy. "They're on their way over here, aren't they?"

"That's right" said the Prince. "One of my contacts inside the force called to warn me that a group of detectives were on their way over here to arrest me."

"Why?" Luke said as the words jumped out of his mouth before he even knew what he was saying"

"They didn't know. They just said that the Police are on their way."

Almost as soon as he said that, one of his Guards called to say that they Police were in the building and on their way up.

"What will you do?" said Mary.

"There's nothing I can do," said the Prince, "but wait here and see what this is all about."

After about five-minutes a group of Police, some in uniform and some in plain clothes, walked into the room without knocking.

With no explanation or chance to respond, one of the Policemen forcefully grabbed the Prince and put him in handcuffs.

"Juan Rodriguez, you are under arrest for the murders of Edmundo Caceres, Juan Hernandez, Salvador Nasrallah and Miguel Colix at La Cantina."

"Based on what?" Luke demanded, but to no avail. The Police continued to arrest the Prince, and they let Luke know in no uncertain terms that if he didn't stay out of their way he could be next.

Paco, the Prince's right hand man had arrived just as they were taking the Prince away. You could see by the look in his eyes that he was both angry and worried.

"Call my lawyer," he said as they were taking him away.

Luke was tempted to intercede, and because of the Mark of the Feathered Serpent, he was confident that he could handle the police. But the Prince gave him a look that said "Don't do it." So they watched as they took him down the hall and out through the elevator to the parking garage where they had a police car waiting to take him to jail.

As soon as the Police were out of the room, Paco jumped on the phone and called the Prince's attorney. He gave them strict instructions to stay out of it and let him handle things, so they waited.

Later on that same morning Luke was to meet with the Mayan Council of Elders to discuss his journey, so he gathered his tattoo bag and took one of the Prince's helicopters to Copan. They landed in the same spot they always used, but unfortunately El Diablo found out about this landing spot and he had four men waiting to kidnap Luke when they landed.

As soon as Luke stepped out of the chopper, four of El Diablo's men stepped out from the heavy jungle foliage and into the clearing. They were armed with rifles, and poured out a heavy concentration of gunfire on the helicopter and killed the pilot. They dragged him out of his seat, then reached over and turned the chopper off. All the while, two men covered Luke with their rifles to ensure that he stayed put.

Luke reached over and punched one of the men who were guarding him. He punched him so hard that he knocked him off his feet. Immediately, he spun around and delivered a roundhouse kick to the other guard, knocking him unconscious. The two men going through the helicopter stopped what they were doing and turned on Luke.

When the third man came within arm's reach Luke grabbed his rifle and pulled it right out of his hands. He was momentarily shocked, but before he had a chance to recover Luke smashed him in the face with the rifle butt and knocked him unconscious.

The last man assessed the situation and decided to shoot Luke while he was still out of reach. Before he could, Luke swung the rifle around like a club and threw it at him. He hit him so hard that he literally knocked him off his feet. In the meantime, the first man that Luke hit got back up, so he struck him several times quickly and put him down again.

The whole fight only took a couple of minutes, and Luke was able to handle El Diablo's thugs without having to kill them, which he was glad about.

He climbed into the van that El Diablo's men had come in and found the keys in the ignition. It turned right over and Luke made his way to the highway and followed the all too familiar road that led from the clearing to the ruins at Copan.

When he arrived he parked the van near the Temple of Kukulcan and walked around to the back entrance. They were expecting Luke and greeted him warmly. There was much ado made over his tattoo. It was very rare.

Luke went into great detail about his journey and the struggles they endured. They were particularly interested in the appearance of Great Fiery Jaguar Paw, and his transformation from man to jaguar.

"Did you bring back the Sacred Stone?"

"Yes" Luke said, "I have it right here." he reached into his tattoo bag and produced the stone that the Ancient King had given him. It was about the size of a golf ball, and the Shamans all took turns holding it and absorbing as much of the stone's power as possible.

"It is the Stone of Transformation," said one of the Shamans. "Once you learn to use the power of the stone, you will be able transform into a jaguar. El Diablo's mind control won't work on the jaguar."

"How will I learn to use the power of the stone?" Luke asked. "And what about the Prince?"

"You will meet Pacal. He wears the Mark of the Feathered Serpent, and he will guide you into transformation. You will leave tomorrow."

"As for the Prince, that will be difficult," one of the other Shamans said. El Diablo has used his ability to control men's minds and caused Chief Gorge to arrest the Prince. He has several witnesses and the Chief is convinced that he's guilty. They've charged him with four counts of first degree murder."

"What can I do?" Luke asked.

"You can defeat El Diablo. Once you do, his power over the Chief's mind will dissipate."

"How can he be defeated? Luke continued. "He'll never surrender. Will I have to kill him?"

"That's one way to get rid of him. But if you can tattoo him with the Mark of Kin, the Sun God, it will block his channel to Ah Puch, and eventually the Mark of the Skull will fade and disappear from his arm."

"How will I find him?"

"He'll find you" one of the Shamans said. "He'll find you."

In the meantime, back at the Penthouse, everyone's attention was focused on getting the Prince released from jail. There was a sense of urgency to get him released before he got transferred to Xibaba prison. But finally, Paco was able to get Colonel Morales to intercede, and the judge agreed to release the Prince in the custody of the Cornel over the objections of Chief Gorge.

While Luke was meeting with the Council of Elders Stacy had been lying down and resting. She was nearly eight months pregnant, and was constantly feeling tired. She was napping when the telephone rang. It was Marti, calling from Miami, and she sounded scared.

"Stacy, is that you?"

"Yes, calm down. What's the matter Honey?"

"They were here."

"Who was there" Stacy said.

"Two men came to the house looking for Luke. They

said he owes them money and that they were going to hurt me if they don't get paid. Do you know these scary men?"

"Yes. What else did they say?"

"They said that they would be back in a week, and if I didn't have their money something bad will happen. What'll I do? You know I don't have any money. All I have is a credit card my Dad left me to use while he was in Honduras. How much do they want?" Marti asked with a shaky voice.

"Twenty thousand dollars," Stacy answered.

"Twenty thousand dollars!" Where are you going to get that much money?"

"I don't know, but I'll think of something. Luke will be back soon, and we'll figure out a way to come up with the money." You just stay home and keep all the doors and windows locked. I'll call you back later."

"Ok. But please do, I'm frightened," Marti said.

Luke made it back to the Penthouse by noon. He opened the door and stepped into the apartment, but before he could even get the door closed Stacy was all over him. She was beside herself with worry.

"Oh Luke, I'm so glad your home. Marti called while you were gone. Tico's men went to her house and threatened her. They want the money. We have to do something."

"Oh my," Luke said. "We came down here thinking we could find the ink and sell it. But by now I realize that the ink is not for sale, so I'm not sure what to do. I can't leave Honduras with El Diablo on the loose, but if we don't, those animals will probably hurt Marti. I need some time to think."

Luke walked back to his bedroom alone and sat in the chair meditating and looking for an answer. He was back there for over an hour when it finally came to him – the lottery. Stacy knows the winning numbers for every lottery before it happens. This idea was a gift from Kukulcan to get us out of this bind and keep us here in Honduras until I could take out El Diablo.

Everyone agreed that this would be the best solution. Uncle Robert was distraught when he heard about the incident, but agreed to let them handle it.

Max coordinated security for Marti. Several members of Jack's security team picked her up and moved her to Jack's house where she would be safer. Stacy would give Jack's men the winning numbers, but only enough to take care of Tico before somebody gets hurt.

The Prince was out of jail and back in the Penthouse by dinner time, thanks to the Cornel. Everyone came together for supper, and they were all taken aback by Luke's tattoo. None of them had ever seen the Mark of the Feathered Serpent before, and they all agreed that it was the most beautiful tattoo they had ever seen.

Later, when they were alone, Stacy and Luke called Marti and told her the plan. She was frightened, but glad to be getting out of the house and over to Jack's place. The lottery would play again in two days, and until then Marti would be safe.

Luke went to bed late that night. He couldn't sleep. His mind was racing. He was worried about Marti and curious for himself. He would be meeting with a man that wears the Mark of the Feathered Serpent and he had a lot of questions. In the morning, Luke was hoping he would get some answers.

The next morning, Luke was packing a few things in his backpack for the journey when Stacy stopped in her tracks. She gave him a very troubled look. "It's the planes; the Columbians have destroyed the Princes airplanes."

"Are you sure? What happened?" Luke asked her.

"I need to tell the Prince," she said and bolted out the door to find him. Luke followed, and eventually they found him in his office."

At almost the same moment they arrived the Prince hung up his phone. With a pained look on his face, he shared the news he had just received.

"There're all gone. The whole hanger has been destroyed. Two of my men were killed."

"EL Diablo," Luke blurted out.

"No," Stacy said. "It's the Columbians."

The Prince looked surprised and said, "How did you know?"

"It's the tattoo, the Mark of Knowledge," Luke said. "It's already started to work on her."

"You are correct," The Prince continued. "It is the Columbians. They think I stole their cocaine shipment."

"We're not safe here," Stacy said. "The Columbians know where we are. They're coming for us."

"I agree," said the Prince. "I will have to deal with them eventually, but we can't sit here and wait for them to hit us. How much time do we have?"

"I'm not sure," Stacy said.

"We can't stay here, and there's almost nowhere in the city that they won't find us," the Prince said. Suddenly he stopped speaking, looked puzzled for a second then blurted out, "I know a place. There's a convent in Santa Rosa. It's hidden away up in the mountains. Nobody ever goes there. Most people don't even know it exists."

"Who are they?" Luke asked.

"It's run by The Sisters of Mercy. They've been there for almost a hundred years providing food and medical care to the children in the area. "There has never been a group of kinder or gentler souls," the Prince said. "They come here as young women and dedicate their lives to the hundreds of Mayan children living in the mountains near the convent. I've been up there to help them a few times. We can go there. We should leave here as quickly as possible. Let's pack enough things for a week and try to leave here within fifteen-minutes."

Everyone ran back to their suites and packed some things as quickly as possible. The Prince already had a backpack prepared for this eventuality. He grabbed it and ran back to his office. He reached under his desk and pushed a button that opened a wall safe behind one of the large murals on his wall. He reached in and pulled out a money bag that he loaded with a large bundle of cash and gold. Once he had filled it to capacity, he closed the top and began to make his way to the roof.

When he got there, two choppers were waiting. Fortunately they were both on the roof of the Prince's building instead of the hanger when the Columbians hit it. Everyone boarded as quickly as possible, and the choppers lifted up and headed out in the direction of Santa Rosa.

Luke began to question himself again for the first time in weeks. *"Why did I bring Stacy to this dangerous place?"*

"Are you okay Stacy?" He asked.

"I'm ok. The babies sure are moving around though."

"I wish we were back in Miami. You're eight months pregnant. We should have gone home a week ago."

"It wouldn't do any good now baby. El Diablo's not going to stop until you give him the Feathered Serpent tattoo, and he'll follow us back to Miami, I just know he will. We need to stay here with the others until you take care of El Diablo and the Prince makes peace with the Columbians."

After a little over an hour, the choppers touched down in a clearing about twenty miles outside of town. Santa Rosa is located high up in the mountains, and the roads are so bad that the normal mode of transportation is by horse or donkey.

Luke was worried about Stacy. In her condition this trip was really hard. Thankfully, the Prince performed a miracle and obtained an off-road jeep with two gas tanks. Gasoline is hard to find in the mountains, and the Jeep had just enough fuel to get to us to Santa Rosa and back.

They made their way up the mountain road on horseback. The Prince rode in front with the guide. Jack and Mary followed, and Stacy rode in the Jeep while Luke drove. The vehicle had been outfitted with extra pillows to help soften the pain of the journey for Stacy, but she was in no condition for a journey like this. Max and Rosa rode behind the Jeep on horseback. Rosa had grown up with horses, but Max had not ridden a horse more than a couple of times in his whole life. Fortunately, Rosa was there to keep him from falling off

After a grueling one-and-a-half-hour trek they finally pulled into Santa Rosa. The Sisters saw them coming and met them at the Gate. They helped Stacy out of the Jeep and into the convent where she was able to lay down.

The Prince was well known to the Sisters because of the charitable work he had done in this part of the country. So, when he arrived; he found a clean bed, a hot meal, and a warm welcome. The Prince hoped we would be safe at the Convent while he figured out how to deal with the Columbians.

After dinner, the Prince sat at a table in the kitchen with Jack and Max. They were enjoying the fine wine the Sisters made right here at the convent, and reviewing options for handling El Diablo. When Luke came in, Jack spotted him and spoke first.

"You're back."

"Where were you Luke?" Max said. "I haven't seen you since dinner."

"I was out in the jungle. I needed some peace and quiet to hear from Kukulkan. He wants me to tattoo Max with the Butterfly of Life."

"What?" Max said.

"You have proven yourself to be a worthy and faithful. You have risked your life to defeat El Diablo, and Kukulcan wants to heal your leg. We will need you to be one hundred percent in the days to come."

"When are you going to do it?" asked Max.

"Whenever you're ready," Luke said.

"I'm ready now." Max replied.

"Good," Luke said. "Tomorrow I will go to Yoro, a city on the river. There is a Warrior there who wears the Mark of the Feathered Serpent. He will be expecting me, so it's good that we do yours tonight."

The Nuns agreed to let Luke do Max's tattoo in the kitchen. Luke asked everyone to leave except Jack, who would assist him. He knew the nuns would never tolerate prayers to Kukulkan. He also knew that he couldn't do the tattoo without the hand of Kukulkan guiding him, so he thought it best to clear the room.

The three of them sat on the ground in a circle. Luke closed his eyes and raised his hands towards the heavens. He began to chant Mayan prayers to Kukulkan, the War Serpent. And as he prayed, heaviness fell on the room, and the presence of Kukulkan filled the place.

Luke turned his head and looked Max straight in the eyes. The spirit of Kukulkan flowed through his body as he spoke.

"Today you will receive the Butterfly of Life. Your courage in protecting the Maya has not gone unnoticed. Kukulcan will heal your legs, and strengthen your body. Be still, and listen. You will hear the voice of Kukulkan speaking to your spirit. Soon you must face the evil one, but have no fear. The hand of Kukulkan will guide you, and you will be a mighty weapon in his hands."

They continued to pray and eventually, the presence of Kukulkan gradually faded and the heaviness lifted.

Luke pressed the needle into Max's skin. Tap, tap, tap with the mallet. He pushed the needle deeper into Max's arm, driving the needle into his body over and over again. The pain was strong, but Max was stronger; and after about thirty minutes, Luke had finished the outline.

They all stood up and took a short break to stretch their legs. Max didn't mind the pain because he knew his newfound abilities would help him protect Rosa. In fact, he had already started feeling something in his legs before the tattoo was even completed.

Over the next hour, Max endured the grueling coloring process. But instead of growing weaker, he got energized as the ink hit his skin. And as the tattoo began to take shape, Max's body seemed to come alive. It was beautiful.

Everyone crowded around to see the completed tattoo. It was identical to the Butterfly of Life tattoos that he gave Tomas in the jungle and the children at La Paz. Luke sat back in his chair and breathed a heavy sigh of relief. He was mentally and emotionally drained. Max, on the other hand, had never felt better.

"Luke, what's happening to me? My whole body feels electric."

"It's the tattoo," Luke said.

Max started to jog back and forth across the full length of the huge kitchen without even breathing heavy. He began to move faster and faster until he was practically running.

When he passed the kitchen door that led outside he stopped momentarily. He looked out and then he glanced over at Jack and said, "You coming?"

"Oh yeah," Jack said as he followed him out the door.

They ran side by side, across the Convent's courtyard and out onto the dirt road that led back down the mountain. It was getting dark outside, and normally the Sisters stayed inside the safety of the Convent walls after dark, but not tonight. Max was blowing it out. His breathing was easy and measured and his leg muscles were pumping like a finely tuned machine.

After they had run about five-miles, they turned around and started running back towards the Convent. As they ran, he and Jack made eye contact. Tears began to swell up in Max's eyes, and Jack understood why. It had been over twelve years since Max had run, and here he was, running as well or better than he did in college. It was magical.

Tomorrow the Prince, Jack, and Max would go with Luke to Yoro. The Prince was still hoping that one of El Diablo's men would sell him out for money. He also hoped that if he had a witness who was willing to tell the truth about what happened at San Miguel, the Columbians might give him an opportunity to prove his innocence.

The next morning, Stacy and Luke were awakened by the sound of church bells. The brass and copper bells rang out in the morning sun, calling the faithful to Mass.

Father McGee had made the same journey he's made twice a week for the past seven years. He travels to the convent to hear confessions and say Mass. He performs the service and gives communion to the nuns, as well as the eighty or so Mayans who show up regularly.

Stacy and Luke made their way down the back staircase that led directly into the kitchen. The smell of homemade bread baking in the oven filled the air, and the smell of fresh coffee served up an invitation to breakfast.

The Sisters were hard at work cooking eggs, sausage, potatoes, fruit, bread, and coffee. Everyone was eating breakfast in the kitchen and reviewing the plans for the day.

"Where's Max?" Luke asked.

"I saw him earlier this morning. He said that he was going out for a run," the Prince said.

"I hope he's okay," Mary said. "He shouldn't push himself too hard."

"He knows his limits," Jack said. "Besides, last night he was on fire. I was having trouble keeping up with him. I haven't seen him run like that since the Notre Dame days."

Just then Max came walking in, covered in sweat and fresh from his run.

"Max, we were worried about you. Where did you go?" Stacy asked.

"It's hard to explain, but when I woke up this morning I felt like running."

"Look, you're not limping anymore," Rosa said.

"I know. And I ran like I've never run before. I'm running better than I did in college."

"It's the tattoo" Luke said.

The more they talked about it, the more you could see the emotion welling up in Max's eyes. He had been one of the greatest running backs in the history of Notre Dame Football. Jack used to say Max's running was pure poetry in motion. But his dreams were taken from him in a matter of moments on a Saturday afternoon in Columbus, Ohio. After the injury, Max was never able to play football again, and he walked with a pronounced limp. But that was before the tattoo. Now, Max had his mojo back.

After breakfast, the guys gathered their stuff together

and prepared to leave. They would travel by horseback and boat, and needed to be back to the convent before dark. Nothing good happens in the jungle after dark.

"Are you going to be okay Mary?" Jack said.

"I'll be fine. The Sisters are going to show us how they make that wonderful bread. We'll have a good day."

"What about you Stacy?" Luke said.

"I don't know. I've got a bad feeling about it, but I'm not sure why. I think somebody knows we're here."

"How can that be? Our guide is the only one who knew we came up here, and he's still with us. Nobody else knows we're here."

"I don't know Luke. I can't tell if it's El Diablo or the Columbians."

"Maybe we're not safe here anymore," he said.

Suddenly, Stacy began to cry.

"This is not how I want my babies to be born. But where can we go? All you can do is meet with Pascal and get whatever it is that he has for you. At least we'll have a fighting chance."

Reluctantly, Luke departed the Convent for Yoro with the Prince, Max and Jack. They followed their guide on horseback up into the high mountains. The trail disappeared at times, but the horses knew the route by heart, and they the riders were simply along for the ride.

They were surrounded by the sights, sounds, and smells of the jungle. Sunlight barely poked through the treetops as they waded through the thick underbrush. The monkeys swung from tree to tree, and the colorful McCaw's flocked overhead. Luke was taken aback by the raw beauty of the place,

After about an hour they came to the Patoka River. Their guide secured the horses in a small pen that had been set up for this purpose. There were boats on the shore, and they all boarded a skinny boat and sailed down the river. Alligators and snakes were in ample supply as they gently glided through the water, and their guide gave them strict instructions to keep their hands in the boat because of flesh eating fish.

They sailed for about thirty-minutes when they came to Yoro, a small village nestled between the river and the jungle. As they pulled up to the shore, the people came out to greet them. They welcomed their visitors and escorted them to a shelter where the Warrior was waiting for Luke. He was invited to enter the tent, but the others were instructed to wait outside.

The Warrior Pacal was an older man whose countenance projected wisdom and strength. His physical stature was that of a much younger man. He stood straight and tall, and his body was well toned. Yet, his hair was gray, and his face carried the lines of age.

He extended his hand and greeted Luke by name. When he did, the first thing Luke noticed was that he wore the Feathered Serpent tattoo. He spoke to Luke in Mayan, and yet Luke understood him and he understood Luke.

He invited Luke to sit down, and he began to pray. The spirit of Kukulcan filled the room, and became so strong that Luke feared it might kill him. They were enveloped in a cloud with electric charges firing within his body. It felt as if he were burning, and just as the feeling was becoming unbearable, it stopped. The presence faded and the room returned to normal.

The Warrior Pacal looked at Luke and said "show me your stone."

He retrieved it from his tattoo satchel and handed it to him.

"The Mayan warrior controls his fighting space," he said. "You're fighting space is the barrier that surrounds your body. The sacred stone will provide a shield of protection for you against the attacks of El Diablo."

"Kukulcan has anointed you for battle. You have already been given all the fighting skills that you will need. Kukulcan will guide you in your battle to defeat El Diablo, and you will prevail against the evil one."

Pacal reached down into his pocket and pulled out a knife. Without warning he tried to stab Luke with it, but he was unable to. Every time the blade got to within a couple of feet of him it simply bounced off an invisible barrier. It was amazing. The Mark of the Feathered Serpent gave Luke fighting skills, and the Sacred Stone gave him a shield of protection. He would be virtually unbeatable.

"Remember" said Pacal. "When you are near El Diablo you will be susceptible to his mind control. You must fight it with every fiber in your body. But if it is defeating you, transform into a Jaguar. The mind control doesn't work on a Jaguar, but you will lose your shield so you must move quickly".

Pacal showed Luke many other things. When it was over, they spent some time with the village elders and visited as many of the families as they could.

Luke was anxious to leave because he was worried about the others who were waiting at the convent. They needed to be home before dark so they said their goodbyes, got back into the skinny boat, and set sail for the Convent.

When they reached the place where they had left their horses, they docked the boat and continued on horseback. The closer they got, the more he felt that something was wrong. When they finally reached the convent, they found the place in complete disarray. The Sisters were crying and praying, trying to come to grips with the tragedy that had occurred.

"What happened here?" Luke asked one of the Sisters.

"El Diablo was here. He wanted you, and when he learned you were not here he went crazy. He tried to make Father McGee tell him where you were, and when he wouldn't, El Diablo beat him over and over again."

"Where is Father McGee?" the Prince said.

"He's resting. Sister Francis is a nurse and she is attending to him."

"Where's Stacy?" Luke asked.

"El Diablo took her," the Nun said.

"What do you mean he took her?" Luke exclaimed.

"She was baking bread when she suddenly stopped and said, "He's coming. Somehow he's found us and he's coming."

She ran out into the jungle to hide with Mary and Rosa, but when El Diablo got here he found them anyway. He took them with him. He said you would know what he wants. He gave me this phone number. He said to tell you to call it if you want to see your wife alive again."

Luke's heart sunk. The words were like a knife in his chest.

"In her condition, she could lose the babies or even die." Luke thought.

Several of the Sisters had bumps and bruises where El Diablo's men had roughed them up. And if there was ever a doubt about what they were dealing with, now all the cards were on the table for everyone to see.

Jack, Max, the Prince and Luke met in the kitchen to consider their options.

"If we don't move quickly, he'll hurt the girls to get our attention," the Prince said.

"I'll turn myself over to him if he'll release Stacy, Mary and Rosa unharmed," Luke said. "He must still think that somehow I can do these tattoos without the blessing of Kukulkan. He must believe that his rogue Shaman has lost his touch," he said. "He's irrational. I don't think he understands that if I do the tattoo it'll bring on the curse without the hand of Kukulkan. And every one of his men that get tattooed will turn into homicidal maniacs."

"I think that even if you turn yourself over to him, he'll kill all four of you anyway," Jack said.

"He's right," said the Prince. "But I think I've got an idea."

He picked up his phone and called Ricardo Garcia, who harbored much animosity towards El Diablo after the raid at San Miguel. He lost fifteen men, and his contract with the Columbians.

The phone rang four, five times before Garcia finally answered.

"Hello."

"Hello. I am Juan Rodriguez."

"Oh yes," he responded. "You're the one they call the Prince of the city. Yes, I know who you are."

"I heard El Diablo owes you about fifty pounds of Cocaine."

"Well, he and I will have a conversation about that very soon."

"Yes. I'd like to speak with him as well," said the Prince." "He has convinced the Columbians that it was I who stole the drugs. Now I need to convince them that it was El Diablo all along. They will know where he is, and if they believe me, they will help me find him."

"Okay. So what do you want?" said Garcia.

"Ten minutes. I want ten minutes to make my case," The Prince said.

"I can probably arrange a meeting with the Columbians" Garcia said. "I have heard that they are very anxious to meet with you. If they believe you, then you will have an ally. If they do not, they'll kill you."

The meeting was arranged for one o'clock the next day. They were trapped at the convent for now because it was much too dangerous to go out into the jungle at night.

Father McGee had been badly beaten, but there was no permanent damage. While El Diablo interrogated the priest, he bragged about having hijacked the cocaine and blamed it on the Prince. So when he knew what was at stake, Father McGee insisted on going back to San Pedro Sula with the Prince to tell the Columbians what El Diablo said and did.

The first daylight this time of year is six-twenty. By six-thirty they headed back down the mountain. We were hoping that even though the Columbians fear no man, they do fear God. Many of them had a strict Catholic upbringing, and despite their lifestyle of drugs, murder, and robbery; they wouldn't harm a priest. So the Prince thought his chances of staying alive were pretty good if he could convince the Columbians that it was El Diablo who stole the drugs, and that's where Father McGee could help. They may not be willing to believe the Prince, but they might believe a Catholic priest.

The Prince had tried to convince the others he should go alone.

"If the Columbians believe me, then I'll send for the rest of you. And if not, at least I'll be the only one to die. They'll kill everybody that's there, but they won't chase you down afterwards. It's me they want."

"I'm going with you," Luke said. "That is non-negotiable. If things do go bad I want be there to help you."

"It's not necessary. If anything happens to me, they're all going to need you more than ever."

"My wife is being held captive by a madman. I'm not going to just sit here and wait to see what happens," Luke said. "I'm going."

"I'm going too," echoed Jack and Max. Eventually the Prince gave in, so we loaded up the Jeep and headed out.

They arrived at the clearing just outside of Santa Rosa where the helicopter was waiting. It took two hours to fly back to the city and the Prince's penthouse. They landed on the roof and were greeted by several of the Prince's men. He turned to Paco, his right hand man, for an update.

"Where are we?" the Prince said.

"The meeting with the Columbians has been confirmed. We'll meet at one o'clock in Father McGee's office at the Cathedral of St. Peter. We'll have four men waiting to escort them in, but once they're in the church they'll be hard to control. There are just too many options. They could strap bombs to their chests and blow us all up, which is what they did in Tegucigalpa. Or they could just walk-in here with guns blazing," Luke said.

TATTOO: The Mark of the Feathered Serpent

"They could simply overpower us and torture me until they get what they want," the Prince added.

"The Columbians insisted the only people in the room for the meeting will be you and one other. Father McGee will be there as well, but with Luke at my side, one other person is all I'm going to need," said the Prince as he made his way to his private suite.

"Ok, it's eleven-thirty right now. I'm going to take a shower and get something to eat before we leave for the church. After all, if I'm going to be killed today, at least I'll be clean."

"Father McGee, why don't you let me show you to your room so you can get some rest and something to eat before the meeting?" Miguel said.

"That sound's good," said the priest, as he nursed his wounds. He had taken a hard beating at the hands of El Diablo.

"Luke, we'll meet in my office at twelve-thirty" the Prince added.

"Yes" Luke agreed, and headed to his suite to clean up and rest; as did Jack and Max.

At the appointed time the Prince, Father McGee and Luke met in the Prince's office. They made their way down the elevator to the parking garage where there was a car waiting for them. They drove to the church and went inside. Father McGee led them down a hallway behind the alter and into his office.

They sat and waited, made small talk, and tried to stay calm and focused. It was important that the Columbians know the truth, that it was El Diablo who stole their cocaine. Luke was confident that he could handle them if things got out of control, but that would only make matters worse. Luke knew that even if he took out the whole group, that they would just send more killers, and keep sending killers until they eventually get them; and the next time they won't listen to reason.

The Columbians were punctual and professional. There were four of them, dressed in business suits and wearing stoic expressions. The Prince stood to greet them as they entered the room and invited them to sit on the couch. They sat across from the killers and waited for them to speak first.

"This is very unusual. Normally we would not waste time listening to you, but we are concerned with getting the right person. My boat's Captain recognized your man Jose. He gave us a message from you. Do you deny that it was Jose?"

"No," said the Prince. "But I do deny that he works for me. Unfortunately, El Diablo has corrupted him, and he's misleading you so that you'll take me out before I can get to him."

"And why should I believe you?"

"I didn't think you would, but I hoped that you would believe Father McGee."

"Tell me Father, who hurt you?" asked the Columbian.

"El Diablo, the evil one."

"What happened?"

"He came to the convent," Father McGee explained. "He was looking for Luke. When he found out that Luke wasn't there, he went mad. He tore the place up. He bragged about stealing your drugs. He beat me and some of the Sisters for information, but we had none to give; so he took Stacy. He said Luke knows what he wants."

"What does he want?" one of the Columbians said.

"He wants the Mark of the Feathered Serpent" Luke answered while trying to stay calm. "It's a tattoo that has deep religious meaning. It endows the wearer with extraordinary physical abilities, and he is willing to kill to get it" Luke said as I raised his shirt sleeve to reveal his tattoo.

"Let's say that I believed you. What would you do?"

"Jack and I will offer to turn ourselves over to El Diablo if he will release our wives," Luke responded. Once we're on the inside, it will be easier to rescue the girls and take him out."

"How are you going to do that?" the Columbian asked.

"A direct assault is our best option," said the Prince. "I expect El Diablo to break his word. So I will offer to meet him in a neutral place with the idea that I'm there to bring Stacy, Mary and Rosa back" Luke said. "He will kidnap us, and keep the girls anyway. But at least when the assault happens, Jack and I will both be on the inside to protect our wives."

"Father, do you believe this to be true?" asked one of the Columbians.

"Yes I do, for I have seen the evil one with my own eyes."

"Very well," said the Columbian. "If Father McGee

believes you, I will believe you."

After the Columbians left, the Prince called his assault team together. The rescue needed to happen that day. Fortunately, the Prince still had two helicopters left, and enough men to launch an assault.

"What if you find that you are vastly outnumbered when you get there? You really have no idea how many men he has," said Father McGee.

"I will have eight men plus Jack, Max and Luke. It will be enough."

By three o'clock, the Prince's assault team had been assembled and briefed. Now they played the waiting game.

Once on the inside, Luke would need a way to signal the Prince to attack; so he consulted Kukulcan, who instructed him to tattoo the mark of knowledge on the Prince. That way, when the time was right to make the assault, he would know.

Luke called the number El Diablo had given him. The phone rang four times before a man with a pronounced Spanish accent answered. He put him on speaker phone so the others could hear as well.

"Good afternoon Mr. Taylor. We have been expecting your call."

"Cut the crap," Luke said. "I want to speak with Stacy."

There was a brief silence on the other end before he handed the phone to Stacy.

"Luke, is that you?"

Luke could hear her voice shaking, and he could tell that she was fighting back tears.

"Are you ok sweetheart?" Luke said.

"I'm scared Luke."

"Have they hurt you?"

"No, but I'm worried about the babies. I'm having cramps."

"Hold on. We're coming to get you."

Suddenly there was shuffling on the other end of the phone.

"Very well Mr. Taylor. Now here's what you're going to do. You will take a flight to Marcella. Then you will take a taxi into town and proceed to 1211 Calle SO. There you will find a blue Dodge truck. The keys are in the glovebox. You will take CA 4 to La Banca. Turn left on Avenida O, and follow it out of town until you reach 4622. There is a dirt road that leads to a house that is set back off the road. Turn into the driveway and proceed towards the house. I will meet your there."

"Make sure you bring our wives" Luke demanded.

"You will be there at five-thirty if you want to see your wives again in one piece" he said, then slammed down the phone.

Jack and Luke took one of the helicopters to Marcella.

They caught a cab into town, picked up the blue truck, and drove to La Banca. They found their way to Avenida O, and followed it out of town until they reached 4622. It was five-thirty.

They turned into the driveway and proceeded towards the house. Luke saw another truck driving straight towards him, but hey both stopped while they were still about twenty-yards apart.

The truck's windows were completely blacked out, so it was impossible to tell if the girls were back there. Both trucks sat motionless for a moment, waiting to see if the other would make the first move. Finally, Jose stepped out of the truck and into the space between the two vehicles.

Luke jumped out of his truck and walked towards him yelling, "Where's Stacy?"

Jose just smiled and said, "She couldn't make it, but she's waiting for you at the ..."

Before he could finish the sentence Luke punched him in the mouth. He hit him so hard that he knocked him over into some bushes before he fell onto the driveway. Almost immediately, Jose jumped back up and did a spinning roundhouse kick that was aimed at Luke's face, but Luke carried The Mark of the Feathered and had the speed to easily avoid Jose's kick. He also had the strength to put him away in a matter of seconds, which he did. Then he reached down, grabbed Jose by the shirt and shook him.

"Now, let me ask you one more time, where's Stacy?"

Jose pushed him back and jumped up. He started to approach Luke, but regained his composure.

"El Diablo wants to see you now, and he wants you in

one piece. But you and I will get the opportunity to finish this conversation later."

"There's no time like the present," Luke said as he approached Jose for another round, but two men stepped out of Jose's truck and pointed rifles at him, which stopped him in his tracks. He knew they wouldn't kill him until El Diablo got his tattoo. But he was concerned that they still might shoot him. And even though the Mark of the Feathered Serpent gave him tremendous speed, he couldn't outrun a bullet. He thought about his shield, but he needed these guys to lead them to their wives so he backed off and bided his time.

The thugs weren't sure what to do with Jack, but they were afraid to kill him until El Diablo had a chance to interrogate him, so they loaded them both into their truck. They went along with it because it was the only way to find the girls.

We were driven for what seemed to be over an hour and eventually arrived at our destination. It was an armed camp, hidden deep in the jungle.

They were led out of the truck and into a tent. El Diablo was sitting behind a desk, and when he spotted Luke, his whole countenance changed. He stood up, smiling from ear to ear, and said "welcome Luke, it's nice to see you again."

"Where's Stacy?"

"She will be by soon enough." El Diablo said.

"I want to see her now," Luke demanded. "I want to see her right now."

El Diablo reached over and knocked Luke off his feet.

But he was fast. He jumped right back up and waded into the criminal with a flurry of punches. He knocked him down, pinned him on the floor, and began choking him.

One of El Diablo's men rushed over and raised his rifle butt to hit Luke over the head, but Jack was there in an instant. He picked up the thug, raised him up in the air and threw him into a group of El Diablo's men who were standing by watching the fight.

El Diablo focused on the chair he had been sitting in and caused it to fly through the air. It hit Luke in the back and almost knocked him out. Luke stumbled for a second and fell into the table and onto the floor. The criminal began to cause numerous items from the tent to lift up off the ground and hurl them towards me: boxes, chairs, books and various projectiles.

He was momentarily overwhelmed by the assault, but he instinctively remembered the sacred stone, and his body shield. He was able to engage the shield with his mind in time to stop several large objects from striking him, and they bounced off him harmlessly.

Jack saw how distracted El Diablo was when he and Luke were fighting, so he picked up a gun that one of the other men had dropped and raised it to shoot the criminal. But before he could get a shot off, the El Diablo sensed it and shot a fireball from his hands. He scored a direct hit on Jack and knocked him back and onto the ground with burns and bruises all over his body.

The evil one turned on Luke and hit him with another round of terrestrial fire. It knocked him back. His body shield kept him from being burned. However, he could tell that it was weakening.

Luke turned around and delivered a fireball at El

Diablo but he met it with another that blocked his shot. They went back and forth with this, and as they did, Luke began to sense that the evil one was in his head, and reading his thoughts. He kept hearing a voice that told him to drop his shield. It was hard to ignore, and he found himself starting to drop the shields before he realized it. El Diablo was winning, and Luke knew that if this kept up, he would overpower him.

Luke remembered what Pacal had said, "If he is defeating you, transform into a Jaguar. The mind control doesn't work on a Jaguar, but you will lose your shield so you must move quickly."

Luke focused as hard as he could while EL Diablo stood over him and prepared to finish him off. At first he didn't think it was going to happen, then suddenly a huge fireball burst and engulfed him in flames. It knocked El Diablo back. However, Luke felt no pain. In fact, it was just the opposite. He felt empowered.

Luke stepped out of the flames. His mind and thoughts seemed normal, but unbelievably, he had transformed into the body of a Jaguar. Everyone in the room was stunned, and several of El Diablo's men ran from the tent screaming in fear.

El Diablo was momentarily taken aback, and then threw another fireball at Luke. He leaped out of the way before it narrowly missed him. He could feel the flame singe his side and he remembered that he had no shield.

Before El Diablo could fire another round Luke leaped upon him and brought him down. He tried to escape by pushing Luke aside as he rolled out from under him, but it did no good. Luke reached out with his paw instinctually and ripped his face open. He winced in pain and held his face as blood dripped through his fingers. Luke could have easily killed him, but didn't.

Luke stepped back into the flames and transformed back into his own body. He quickly grabbed his tattoo bag and began to outline the Mark of Kin tattoo directly over his skull tattoo. He was able to work at top speed, and as he did, the skull began to recede. The whole thing took less than ten minutes, and by the time he was finished, it had completely disappeared. His powers also disappeared. When he lost his skull tattoo he lost his connection to Ah Puch.

Luke had been given hand cuffs, and was able to restrain El Diablo. However, he was still bleeding heavily; and moaning in pain; so Luke allowed one of his men to attend to him. Suddenly a man walked into the tent dragging Stacy by the arm. He had a gun pressed up against her head. He pointed his pistol in the air and fired it. Everyone immediately stopped what they were doing and looked up.

When Luke spotted Stacy he ran to her. He pushed her guard out of the way and took her in his arms before the guard knew what was happening.

"Oh Luke," was all she could say. Her body was shaking and she couldn't stop crying. Tears flowed down her cheeks, and Luke's rage burned red hot.

"Stacy, are you ok?"

"No, I'm having bad cramps. It hurts. There's something wrong."

While the fight was raging, the others were waiting in a clearing about ten miles from the camp. Because Luke had tattooed the Mark of Knowledge on his shoulder, the Prince was able to follow the events as they unfolded. So when Luke started fighting with El Diablo the Prince looked up at Mike and said, "Let's do it."

"Aye Captain," he said. "We'll give them something to remember you by." So he kicked it into high gear and took off at top speed.

When they arrived on the scene, they set their plan into motion. Mike would cause a distraction while the other chopper would land their team at the opposite end of the camp.

Mike pointed the nose down and did a pass through the camp with guns blazing. He was careful not to hit any of the tents for fear of hurting Stacy or Mary; but he created quite a distraction. El Diablo's men totally missed the second chopper. Mike had caused such pandemonium, that by the time his men saw the rest of the assault team it was too late.

The Prince and two of his men came rushing into the tent where Stacy and Luke were, and El Diablo's men dropped their weapons and surrendered.

Jack limped over to where El Diablo was being treated for his face wounds. He grabbed him by the neck and began chocking the life out him.

"Where's Mary? Where's Mary?" he screamed at the

top of his lungs.

"She's in another tent with Rosa on the far side of the camp," Stacy said, "by the trucks." So the Prince and Luke ran out the door and across the camp until we came up behind the tent Mary was in. Luke leaped over it, and came down on top of the two thugs that were guarding the entrance. He grabbed them both, and smashed their heads together so hard that they fell to the ground unconscious.

Luke rushed into the tent, with the Prince close behind, but they stopped short when he saw that Mary was being held at gunpoint.

The two guards inside the tent were afraid for their lives, and held the gun to Mary's head as an insurance policy. But Luke was unfazed. He stepped across the tent and picked up a machete that was on the ground and asked the Prince to translate for him.

"Tell these two that if they harm Mary, I'm going to tie then up and torture them over a period of a couple of days until they beg for death."

The Prince looked at Luke in a peculiar way. He had never heard the gentile Luke Taylor talk like that, but he delivered the message verbatim.

"Tell them if they let her go, and walk away right now, I'm going to let them live."

So the Prince delivered the message, and it seemed to have an effect, because the two let go of Mary and slowly started to back out of the tent. Suddenly, the Prince fired on them so quickly that he was able to kill both of them before they knew what happened.

"I heard the voice of Kukulkan. They were going to

shoot us as they backed out of the tent," the Prince said. "And I don't feel like getting shot today."

"Me either," said Mary as she held on to Luke. She was still trembling from the ordeal of being kidnapped.

"Excuse me," the Prince said as he exited the tent. "You guys stay here. I need to finish cleaning up this mess."

Chapter 31

The Prince prowled the camp looking for survivors. Two of his ten men were dead, and another three had been wounded.

El Diablo's crew had been decimated. There were seven dead and six wounded, including El Diablo himself. Some of his men had fled into the jungle to escape Mike's guns, but because the jungle was so dangerous at night, they began to walk back into camp and surrender.

When Luke made his way back to the tent where Stacy was, he stopped dead in his tracks. She was sitting in a chair, crying and reeling from cramps. She called out for him and he rushed to her side.

"Luke, Luke. There's something wrong."

"Hold on baby. We'll get you on the chopper and get

you to a hospital."

"I think it's too late for that now," Mary said as stepped into the tent. "She's having those babies right now."

"No. It's too soon," Stacy said.

"Oh my!" said Mary. "Her water broke."

"No, no," Stacy said over and over again.

Suddenly, Mary got a look at Jack and screamed. He was badly burnt, and barely conscious; and she ran to him and took him in her arms.

Luke gently laid Stacy on the ground, and sent the Prince to find a bed for her. He was able to find a large cot that had a mattress; so he picked it up and carried it back to the tent where Stacy was. They laid her on the cot and tried to make her comfortable. She looked up into Luke's eyes and panic overtook her.

"I don't think I can do this baby," she said.

"Sure you can, honey. Women have been doing this for thousands of years. You're going to do fine." Mary said as she continued to rock Jack in her arms.

"Have you ever done this before?" Stacy asked.

"Yes," Mary said. "I spent a whole semester working in the delivery room at University Hospital when I was in Nursing School. And I've been in the delivery room with several of my friends when they had their babies. So don't you worry, everything will be fine."

Luke stepped away for a second and walked over to where Mary was sitting. He whispered in Mary's ear.

"Give it to me straight Mary, how bad is this?"

"I'm worried, but don't you let her know it. She's going to need every ounce of courage she can muster. Those babies aren't quite ready to be born yet. At eight months, their lungs haven't had a chance to fully develop."

"Will they live?"

"If we were in Miami, and these babies were in the neonatal unit at Miami General, their odds would be good. But here in the jungle, I don't know. Even if they survive the birth, they'll die in a couple of hours without oxygen."

Stacy moaned in pain with each contraction.

"Her contractions are getting closer together. Those babies are coming," Mary said.

Stacy was screaming at this point, and the pain was overwhelming her. She had only been in labor for three hours, but when the time came, Mary helped with the delivery, and Stacy pulled through like a pro.

Mary caught each one, first a girl and then a boy, but they were sick. They were very sick.

It had been just as Mary said; the babies struggled for each breath and Stacy was getting weaker by the minute from loss of blood. Luke looked to Mary for some direction.

"She needs to be in a hospital. How soon before she can travel?" Luke asked.

"She shouldn't go anywhere in this condition," Mary said. "She's lost too much blood."

"Give the babies a tattoo," Max suggested.

"Maybe I could," Luke said and walked out of the tent. "I'll be back."

"Where's he going?" asked Max.

"I don't know," said Mary, and then turned her attention back to Stacy and the babies.

"Luke, where're you going?" Max said.

"I'll be right back!" Luke insisted as he walked outside.

He stepped into the jungle and walked far enough that he couldn't see the camp anymore. He sat on the ground and began to meditate and chant Mayan prayers. He closed his eyes and called out to Kukulkan to show him his will. Soon, heaviness fell upon the jungle, and the presence of Kukulkan filled the place.

Luke felt his whole body being raised off the ground, and the voice of Kukulkan spoke to his spirit.

"Son of Pasah, Your wife will receive the Butterfly of Life, but your children will not survive the tattoo. There is another way. You are to tattoo the children with the Mark of the Star, and I will guide your hand. Once the tattoo is complete, it will disappear, and the children will be whole. But the tattoo is like a seed. When the children begin to mature, more tattoos will appear and they will be a powerful tool in your hands".

Luke continued to pray until the presence of Kukulkan faded and the heaviness lifted.

He ran back to the camp and into the tent where Stacy and the babies were. He opened his tattoo bag and reached for a needle; but Kukulkan stopped him and guided his hand to a different tool. Once he had the correct needle, he reached for the ink, and Kukulkan guided his hand again.

Stacy held the baby girl in her arms as Luke positioned the needle, and Kukulkan showed him how to tap the needle gently with his finger, just hard enough to plant the seed.

As soon as he did, a beautiful blue star appeared on the child's arm. It radiated outwards, and brought everything it touched to life. Her skin began to glow as the seed flowed through her body. Her breathing became steady, and her pulse was strong. She began to cry, and so did Stacy. Her baby was going to live.

Then it was the boy's turn, and the same miracle happened.

Finally, Luke knelt down beside his wife. He kissed her gently on the head, and began giving her the Butterfly of Life tattoo. As he completed each piece of the tattoo, Stacy looked noticeably better. And by the time he was finished, you would have never known that she had just given birth to twins.

The Prince loaded Luke, Stacy, and the twins into the first helicopter; along with Jack, Mary, and Max. They left EL Diablo tied up and under armed guard. The second chopper stayed behind with some of the Prince's men until Colonel Morales of the Honduran Military could pick up the prisoners and clean up the mess.

The helicopter carried us away, over the jungle, and in the direction of home. Luke wasn't even sure he knew where home was anymore, but he did know that they would be coming back to Honduras. This place had become a part of them, and they were part of it.

TATTOO

El Diablo's Revenge
Book 2 of the Tattoo Series

The following preview of the next book in the series is provided for your reading pleasure. I hope you enjoy!

Preview

"The world is a dangerous place to live, not because of the people who are evil, but because of the people who don't do anything about it."

— Albert Einstein

Xibalba Prison in Honduras is hell on earth. Never in the history of humanity has there been such a vile collection of human trash crowded into such a small space. Beatings, rapes, and even murders are daily activities in Xibalba, *"the place of fear."*

The prisoners run the prison. The guards provide essentials, like food and water, but have locked the prisoners in and allowed them to self-govern. The strong survive and lord over the weak, but the system runs smoothly for the Honduran military that oversees the whole operation and doesn't care if the prisoners kill each other.

Xibalba is laid out like a small city with streets, shops, food vendors and various dwellings the prisoners live in. During the day, groups of inmates line the streets of the prison, sitting on wooden benches with nowhere to go and nothing to do. Family visits are encouraged, and the prison gets a daily stream of women and children who have come to visit their loved ones. Conjugal visits are also allowed, but privacy is hard to come by.

Jose *"El Toro"* Morales ran Xibalba prison from the inside until El Diablo arrived. There was a brief disagreement about who would be in charge, but the next morning the Military guards found El Toro's body. His throat had been sliced from ear to ear, and his lifeless corpse thrown over the fence, but not before every tooth in his mouth had been extracted by hand with a pair of plyers. Message delivered, message received.

The next morning El Diablo was up and out early. As he stepped into the morning sunlight he cast an ominous shadow. Standing nearly seven feet tall, his long black hair hung to his shoulders. He wore blue jeans and a wife beater t-shirt. His steeled toed boots looked more like weapons then shoes, and the prison tattoos that covered his body made him a terrifying sight.

As he strolled through the prison yard the other prisoners huddled together in small groups. They spoke in hushed tones and looked away quickly if El Diablo looked their direction. His reputation was well known in the prison from his previous stay.

No one dared speak to or make eye contact with him until Fernando found him in the yard and greeted him. Fernando had worked for El Diablo on the outside and had earned his trust.

"Good morning boss. I would welcome you back, but I don't think you are very happy to be here."

El Diablo turned his head just enough to snarl at Fernando while never taking his eyes off the yard. His face and head were heavily bandaged. He carried the war wounds from his fight with Luke in the jungle. Luke had mauled his face when he transformed into a Jaguar. It had taken over a hundred stiches to close his wounds. The injuries left El Diablo with severe facial scaring. He had been in the hospital for a week before he was finally transferred to the prison, and the whole time he had one thought – kill Luke Taylor.

The gambling and the drug traffic in Xibalba had been run by *El Toro*, but there was a new sheriff in town. El Diablo would bring the players into line all at once.

"Did you deliver my message?" El Diablo said.

"Si, they will report to you in your office when you are ready." Fernando replied.

"Tell them I'm ready" he said.

He walked back through the yard towards his newly acquired residence. He had commandeered El Toro's place. It had been his residence the last time he was there. It was a six- room suite with a view of the mountains and fit for a prison king. As jailhouse boss he literally ruled the roost and decided how much space each inmate would get. For those who were able to get money from the outside, the system worked well because they could afford to pay the rent that El Diablo demanded. But for everyone else, they crammed themselves into small cells and dared not complain.

When he was still some distance from his residence he passed a crowd of inmates who were watching two large thugs beating a young man who looked to be little more than a teenager. The boy was laying on the ground, while his attackers stood over him - kicking him in the ribs, and beating him with sticks. He was bleeding, and it was plain to see that he was unable to get up and defend himself.

El Diablo walked over to investigate. When the men who were beating the youth saw him they stopped what they were doing and cleared a path for him. He knelt down on one knee beside the young man, who was only partially conscious, and examined him momentarily. Then he looked up at one of the thugs who had been beating him and asked him directly.

"Why are we beating this puppy?"

"He owes protection money, but he can't pay, so we are making an example out of him."

"I see" El Diablo replied. "And why is he here?"

The young man looked up at El Diablo with a bloody face and answered the question.

"I came down here on Spring Break. I got caught with a small bag of pot in my luggage when we went through customs and they sent me here."

"For how long?" El Diablo asked.

"Five years" said the young man in a muted whisper.

"His parents send him money, but it's never enough"

said one of the thugs.

El Diablo put his hand on the young man's shoulder.

"What's your name?"

"Ricky" the young man replied.

"Well Ricky, you're never going to survive in here. From now on you work for me."

As he spoke, he looked directly at the two thugs who had been beating the young man and they both got the message loud and clear. From then on, Ricky was untouchable.

The gang leaders from throughout the prison reported to El Diablo as ordered. There were four men who controlled vise in Xibalba, and they came to El Diablo's place to get their instructions. However, El Diablo wasn't concerned about vise. He needed their help to make his escape.

His plan was set. He would wait for the prison supply truck to arrive on Friday and create a diversion to distract the guards while he walked right out the front door.

The prison was surrounded by a sixteen-foot metal fence with razor wire at the top. There were six guard towers which encircled the prison and allowed the guards complete coverage of the facility. Once inside the gate there's a fifty-foot buffer space and a second inner fence, just as tall and with the same razor wire.

The procedure is always the same. The supply truck

pulls up to the front gate and is allowed inside the first of the two fences. Once inside, the fence is closed behind the truck and the inner fence is opened to give the supply truck access to the Prison. The truck pulls up to the storehouse and the prisoners unload it. The Military believed that they had very little to worry about. The few times that prisoners had tried to hi-jack the truck or mount an escape the guards would force everyone inside with machine gun blasts from the guard towers. Certain death awaited any prisoner who dared to venture out into the yard, and it didn't take long before the guards were able to starve the prisoners into submission. But this time was different.

"I'm not staying here," El Diablo began. "I'm leaving on Friday afternoon when the supply truck arrives. When the Captain of the Guard opens the inner gate he's going to leave the outside gate unlocked. When he does, everyone will pour out of their cells at the same time."

"It's important that when the lock opens all the prisoners come out of their cells at once" he continued. "I will create a distraction and disarm the guard towers. When I do, everyone will storm the front gate. In the confusion, we'll simply open up the gate and walk out."

"If everybody rushes the gate at the same time, we will be hard to stop" one of the four repeated, denoting agreement.

El Diablo finished handing out instructions for the escape but didn't address day to day activity in the Prison. He wasn't planning to be there long enough to care.

Later that evening his rogue Shaman visited him in prison. He was able to gain entry because El Diablo had bribed the guards. After Luke had mauled El Diablo in the jungle that night he was able to remove the Mark of the Skull tattoo that Ah Puch had given him. It broke his link with the evil one and took away his power to control men's minds. He could no longer levitate objects or fire off energy blasts. The Shaman knew that he would need his powers to pull off his escape plan, and he had come to the prison that night to summon the demon Ah Puch.

The Shaman and El Diablo sat on the floor across from each other and began chanting prayers to Ah Puch, the Lord of Death. They used ancient Mayan incantations to summon the evil spirit into their midst. They continued for some time, growing more intense as they went along. As they prayed, a chill began to set in. Soon it was cold enough to see your breath, and both the Shaman and El Diablo knew the cold was a sign that Ah Puch would soon make his presence known.

Eventually, a smell could be detected. It was a vile stench like rotting flesh. It quickly became so strong that it was difficult to tolerate. Slowly, the evil one materialized. His body was a skeleton with the head of an owl, and his bones rattled as he moved. The tiny bells which were tied to his head feathers made a tinkling sound. But the worst part was the smell. It was the smell of death.

He spoke in a raspy tone that could turn a man's blood cold. His voice was evil, and just the sound of it made El Diablo's skin crawl. He spoke in an ancient tongue, and the

Shaman translated.

"Gold awaits you at the temple of Kukulcan in the ancient city of Altan. There you will find the holy books of the K'iche' Maya. You will take the gold and destroy the books. Then you will have your revenge."

"Yes" El Diablo agreed. "Luke Taylor must die."

The demon moved towards El Diablo accompanied by the cadence of rattling bones and tinkling bells. He reached out with his boney fingers and touched El Diablo's shoulder. When he did, the criminal was hit with a jolt that felt like a bolt of lightning. His arm burned like fire, and as he looked down he could see that Ah Puch had reapplied the Skull tattoo to his shoulder.

Ah Puch stepped back slowly, and just like he materialized, he faded away with the sound of the tinkling bells being heard in the distance.

The Shaman looked at El Diablo with a confused expression on his face. Every Mayan child had heard the story of Pox K'awill, the great Mayan War Lord who defeated the Spanish and stole the gold. But until today, he never heard the location of the gold. It was in Altan, the lost city. The gold would go a long way to funding the criminal's activities. But finding it would be another thing. He would need a plan, and the Shaman had one.

"Luke Taylor will return to Honduras" he began. "He will learn about the gold and the holy books. He is being led by Kukulcan. Once he finds the gold you will turn his own people against him. They will betray him into your hands and lead you to the treasure. Then you will destroy him."

The Shaman and El Diablo plotted and schemed for over an hour to fine tune their plan. When they were finished, they celebrated by finishing off a bottle of tequila and most of a second one. Now the only thing they could do was wait.

The next three days went by uneventfully. El Diablo spent the time reviewing his escape plan with his captains and waited.

When Friday finally arrived, he put his plan into action. He was in a good mood that morning, knowing that he would be free before the day was over. He ate a full breakfast and packed a few things he would take with him.

Later that morning he met with Ricky. The youth was an easy mark for El Diablo, who used his mind control to make him obey his every command. Ricky would play an integral role in the criminal's escape plan by causing a diversion that will allow El Diablo to launch a prison riot. He had smuggled a gun into the prison and gave it to Ricky. He made sure the youth knew how to use it and outlined Ricky's role in the escape.

"When the supply truck pulls up to the warehouse, you'll kill the driver and climb into the truck. Shoot any guard who tries to stop you. Then you will turn the truck around and drive it into the fence."

In his spirit, Bill balked at the idea of murder, but his mind was being controlled by El Diablo and he was powerless to resist.

At three o'clock the supply truck pulled up in front of the prison gate, right on schedule. The driver spoke with one of the Military guards who cleared him to pass and the section chief unlocked the front gate. The truck pulled into the holding area and the gate slowly closed behind him.

El Diablo began to use his mind control to get inside the section chief's head. He started before the gate was even opened. He kept planting the thought in the guards mind to leave the gate unlocked. El Diablo spoke in his mind to the guard over and over, "leave the gate unlocked … leave the gate unlocked." Over and over he chanted until the gate closed. But the guard never switched the lock back on, and nobody noticed.

Finally, the inner gates slowly swung open as the supply truck lumbered into the prison. When it did, El Diablo set his plan into action. He gave the signal for Ricky to approach the truck. The youth made his way from his cell to the storehouse where the truck was being unloaded. He walked over to the driver's side of the vehicle, and without any warning, fired into the cab and killed the driver. Another guard who was standing nearby returned fire and shot Ricky in the leg as he was climbing into the truck. The youth winced in pain but was able to turn around and kill the second guard before he could get off another round.

The sound of gunfire quickly got the attention of every guard in the prison. They rushed to the yard to find Ricky turning the truck around for a run at the fence. Before he got very far, the solders in the guard towers opened fire on the truck and hit Ricky multiple times. He lost control of the vehicle and crashed it into the storehouse. When he did, that was the signal for the other prisoners to rush the gate.

It was complete pandemonium. The guards who had hurried to confront the truck were now being overrun by the deluge of prisoners who were pouring out of their cells and into the yard.

The soldiers who were manning the guard towers opened fire and began killing the prisoners to clear the yard. Meanwhile, the flood of humanity rushed the unlocked gate. The guards in the two towers closest to the front gate began firing down on the prisoners who were escaping, but El Diablo was able to reach into their minds and cause them to begin fighting amongst themselves. The fighting was so intense that they stopped firing on the prisoners and began trying to kill each other.

Because the gate was unlocked, the rush of prisoners pushed it open. Dozens of inmates, along with El Diablo, flooded out into the streets before the guards could regroup.

Now he was free. Now El Diablo would have his revenge.

Book 2 of the Tattoo Series
Coming Spring 2020

ABOUT THE AUTHOR

Juan Bútto began writing at an early age. Fresh out of high school he toured the nation with a rock group where he wrote multiple songs, as well as recorded several albums and videos.

After college, he entered the world of advertising where he spent over twenty years developing creative marketing campaigns for major companies nationwide.

He currently lives in Orlando, Florida with his wife and children.

If you liked this book, please leave a review on the site where it was purchased. Also, find out when the next exciting release is available by joining the email list at SouthCoastPublishingCo@gmail.com

SouthCoast

Publishing Company
(407) 571-9564
SouthCoastPublishingCo@gmail.com

genavisionproductions@gmail.com

CPSIA information can be obtained
at www.ICGtesting.com
Printed in the USA
LVHW112228290123
738193LV00005B/99